I0763526

The Farmer & His Wife

THE FARMER

&

His Wife

Black and White Publishing LLC.

Hardcover printing linked with online musically enhanced edition. Printed in the United States of America

ISBN: 978-1-7367529-0-6

Published by Black and White Publishing LLC., Lockport, New York

The Christian Seder Service was written by Judy Dickinson and used with her permission. All Biblical references are NRSV.

Chapter heading graphics/recipe cards/graphics for nature journaling pages are the property of Canva and used through a subscription.

A whimsically told tale of the Farmer and his Wife as they find and settle their farm.

This book is

DEDICATED

to

The Farmer's Wives who have come before me and patiently led me by the hand, showing and sharing their wisdom in this, our high calling: Bobby. Becky. Betty. Tawna. Carol. Bessie. Cynthia. Mrs. Murphy.

And to Jessica, although not a Farmer or a Farmer's Wife, you listened to the tales of both, and encouraged them to be put down on paper, leading to this, our stories. Thank you.

Table of Contents

Appendixes

Illustrations

Chapter One: The Heist

Some people live in cities, others in towns. The Farmer and his Family live in a Village, but it is getting too tight for them. You see, they have neighbors—they are lovely people, but people in general are not what they seek. They want land, lots of land, teaming with gardens and orchards and every kind of animal to fill it. They want a Farm. You see, they are Farmers already, have been for ever so long. A Farmer isn't something you become. It's something you are. Just like you don't become a baker or a candlestick maker. You are born one. And they were born Farmers.

The Farmer and his Wife even met on a farm. Have you heard that story already? Oh. So you know it. They met on a farm and now here they are, living in a Village. They do their best with what they have. They planted a few fruit trees, and a nut tree or two; they even have a garden, complete with a pumpkin teepee at the end where they read stories and drink tea. It's nice, but in a for now kind of way. Their Farmer's blood itches for more.

But we're getting ahead of ourselves. Let us have the proper introductions, shall we? You know the Farmer, surely, that's why you've come. You want to hear his stories. But have you met his Wife? And the young ones? They're all here. The Farmer's Wife is gathering and sorting the eggs, while Mikaela's in the house, her head stuck in a book. Jacob's over there, in the tree house the Farmer and his Wife built last summer. Hannah's just where you'd expect her to be—off riding bikes with the neighbors.

She loves it here in the Village, which is quite strange. Of all three children, Farmer's blood runs thickest in her. Isn't she the one who pushes that chicken on a swing? And didn't she name each one? There they are now, all in a line. They're looking for her. You can tell by the way they cock their heads to the side like that. That's how they look for her.

The chickens—they're the ones who start all this. To be fair, it isn't their fault. They simply do what chickens do. They lay eggs. Surely, they have no idea that these *particular* eggs on this *particular* day will change everything—how dare you suggest it! Why? Do you see their heads tilted to the side, looking for Hannah again? Yes, it is certain those chickens have been getting rather devious as of late, but to suggest they plotted this whole thing just to get Hannah to themselves is preposterous! We will not even discuss it. They lay their eggs and that is that.

The neighbors arrive, as neighbors so often do. Only on this day they stop at the coop. Did the chickens call them? One can never tell. It certainly is possible. But that simply will not do. That is a Guess. Let us focus only on Facts. And the Facts are this: On every other day, the neighbors pay that coop no mind, but today they stop. They stop and peer into the coop and see a fresh warm egg. They take it. And what does one do with a fresh, warm egg? Why, throw it at the side of the coop, of course. It is simply the way it is done. At least that's what those who know about such thing say. That's how it happens, anyway. They take warm egg after warm egg and smash them against the coop.

The chickens watch, heads tipped to the side. Do you see that one smile? Yes, a smile indeed.

And so, the stage has been set. The Farmer arrives home and sees his coop, the one he made from those pallets he brought home from work—you remember, don't you? You remember how carefully he pulled out each nail, knowing that leaving them would hurt one of his chickens-to-be? Now, the Farmer *must* know that warm eggs are to be thrown, but that doesn't seem to make any difference. He simply shakes his head and says, "This place is too tight for us."

His Wife sighs, knowing he is right. "The house isn't ready to sell," she says, reminding him of the roof that needs fixing.

The Farmer gets right to work fixing this and that. It won't be long, and they will be ready to call the company that sells houses and tell them to sell theirs.

And that's just what they plan to do, honest it is, at least until the letter comes.

It's a normal letter, typed on normal paper, and this is what it says:

Dear Neighbor,

I noticed what a fine job you're doing fixing up your house. My dad likes it, especially. He would like to live there, if you don't mind.

From,

Your Neighbor from the Next Road Over

The Farmer's Wife runs and shows the Farmer the letter. He reads it twice. "Can you believe it?" he asks in wonder. Just then a chicken walks by, head tipped to the side.

The chicken believes it.

Chapter Two: The Want List

The Farmer calls a family meeting, which, of course, is an absolute necessity. Family meetings help decide things and can you think of a bigger decision than buying a Farm?

There's nothing bigger than that!

They meet around the picnic table on the back deck, under the pergola, where clusters of grapey-smelling grapes hang over their heads. Now surely you're thinking, it's a grape, all grapes smell like grapes, but that's just not true. The Farmer and his Wife *only* grow grapes that smell and taste like actual grapes and that's that.

A chicken perches itself on the bench next to Hannah to see what is to become of this. Hannah strokes its feathers lightly.

"We're here to discuss what we want on our Farm," the Farmer begins, but he doesn't need to. Ideas are already gushing like Niagara Falls.

"I want a pool, a big pool with a waterslide," says one.

The Farmer's Wife quickly jots that down on the paper in front of her.

"And my own room," says another, nudging a pesky little brother's foot off her own.

"And I want a Farm kitchen," the Farmer's Wife adds, penning that in. "With a garden just outside the back door."

"I want to stay here. This is our home."

The chicken looks up at Hannah in concern. Silence settles on the group. The Farmer is the one to break it. "I want a barn, a huge barn with lots of room for all my tools."

“Don’t you mean toys?” the Farmer’s Wife asks lightly. The Farmer loves anything with a motor.

His eyes shine, picturing dirt bikes, four-wheelers, snowmobiles, a jet ski or two...

“Alright,” she interrupts before the Farmer can spend too much imaginary money. “We made an appointment with the company that sells houses for tomorrow morning. We’ll give them the list and they’ll find us our Farm.”

The chicken leans against Hannah’s chest, cooing. It likes the sound of that.

Chapter Three: No More Farms

Did you know they can sell out of farms? Well, it turns out they can, because that's just what happened, and this is how it went:

"There are no more farms for sale," the woman behind the desk says.

The Farmer looks at his Wife and together they turn back to the woman. "What? Is that possible?"

"Oh, yes," the woman who works for the company that sells houses says. "It happens all the time. Just last week we ran out of houses all-together."

“No more houses?” the Farmers Wife whispers. Where will they live? Will the little ones have nothing but the stars for their roof and the morning dew for a blanket?

“Oh, don’t worry. There are more for sale now. But not last week. Last week there were none at all.”

The Farmer’s Wife swallows deeply. They have already told the Neighbor from the Next Road Over that her dad can move into theirs! The Farmer’s strong hand settles on her back.

The woman who works for the company that sells houses gets to her feet. The Farmer and his Wife get to theirs. “My advice: Give it a week. There might be all sorts of Farms for sale then.” With that she walks to the door and opens it, wanting them to leave. The Farmer’s Wife bends down and picks up the list she’d set on the chair next to her.

They leave in silence.

Chapter Four: The Open House

There are Farms, and there are places that *could* be Farms. Now, I know you were told that all the Farms were gone, and they were. For three weeks straight the Farmer calls the woman who works for the company that sells houses to check if there are any Farms for sale and each week she says the same thing: There are no Farms left.

The fourth time they call, she says something different. She suggests they look at some houses that *could* be Farms.

So, that's just what they do.

For the first one, they all go. The Farmer and his Wife sit in the front seat, with all three kids crammed in the back.

The house is on a quiet road with a creek running at the end of it.

“My friend Sydney lives on this road,” a voice interjects quietly from the back seat.

The Farmer’s Wife turns to look at Hannah. A picture fills her mind…

Sydney and Hannah riding bikes up and down the quiet road, spending late nights on porch swings, whispering hopes and dreams between giggles and sweet tea…

The truck comes to a stop. “We’re here,” the Farmer says.

Jacob peers out his window. “Is this our new house?”

“Maybe!” the Farmer’s Wife says as she jumps out.

Tea parties and sleepovers, dances and crushes…

The Farmer’s door opens and slowly closes. The Farmer’s Wife turns back to look at him. He isn’t looking at her. His eyes are locked on the house. On the porch. Her eyes go there, too.

The picture of two girls fades, replaced by sagging stones and hanging beams.

Jacob bounds past the Farmer, racing for the porch. The Farmer's protective arm grips him and pulls back. "Woa—better not go that way."

The stairs he'd been racing toward are crumbling. Along with the rest of the porch. It's sinking into the ground, trying to take the house with it.

"Maybe it's just the outside," the Farmer says to his Wife, whose face matches that porch—sunken and dejected. "Let's try the back door," he says to everyone else, leading the way. They silently follow.

The woman who works for the company that sells houses is standing by the back door, waiting for them. Her smile is big and bright. "There are three bedrooms," she says, opening the door.

"Not four?" the Farmer's Wife asks. The computer had said there were four. One for each child, with one left over for a Farmer and his Wife.

"No." Still smiling.

"And a pool?" a child asks.

"No pool."

"And no barn?" the Farmer asks.

"There's a garage," the woman who works for the company that sells houses says. "You could turn that into a barn."

The Farmer's Wife frowns. Animals won't like that very much. They'll always wonder if the family wouldn't rather have just had a car and trade a few of them in for one or three.

The Farmer's Wife looks around the tiny kitchen. It might work. If she really, really tries. "Let's look upstairs," she offers. "Maybe the bedrooms are big."

The woman who works for the company that sells houses leads the way. The first bedroom is tiny.

"Maybe this is meant to be an office," the Farmer says.

"I hope not," the woman laughs. "It's the biggest one!"

The Farmer's Wife looks at the Farmer. The Farmer looks at her.

"What does this door lead to?" the Farmer asks.

All turn to a small door at the end of the hallway. Maybe the woman who works for the company that sells houses had been wrong—maybe this was the missing bedroom! The Farmer's Wife opens the door. A staircase that goes steeply upwards meets them there.

The attic.

An attic can be good—they can fix it up into the bedroom they need!

The stairs creak and groan under the weight of the Farmer and the five others who follow him.

All freeze as sunlight pours down on their faces.

The woman who works for the company that sells houses steps past them to have a look for herself. A bright sunbeam spills across her face. She squints and shades her eyes with her hands. "This is not the house for you!" She is no longer smiling. "The only thing keeping us dry right now is because it's not raining outside!"

All of them look up. It's true. There is nothing but open sky above them.

The Farmer's Wife leans toward the Farmer. "I didn't know you can have a house without a roof."

"You can't," he says and turns to head back downstairs. All follow: down the attic stairs, down the stairs by the three tiny bedrooms, out of the house, and into the truck to go home.

"So, that isn't going to be our house?" Jacob asks.

"No!" they all answer. It's a terrible, terrible house.

The Farmer looks at his Wife before turning back to him. "Don't worry. We'll find just the right spot for our family."

Chapter Five: God's Fingerprints

The Farmer and His Wife go alone to see the next house. And the next one. None of them are their Farm.

"Here's one," the Farmer says one night while he's looking at his computer screen.

His Wife rushes over. "Is it brick? Stone? How many fireplaces are there?"

She looks past him toward the screen. It is a newer house. Not brick. Not stone. And there are no fireplaces.

The Farmer looks up at her. It's him who wants a new house, not his Wife. She likes the old kinds, the ones with squeaky floors and whistling drafts. The ones with stories of their own to tell.

She looks at the screen again. "Are those houses?" In the picture there is a row of houses, sitting right in front.

The Farmer nods.

"No," she answers. "No more neighbors."

They see more houses, lots of them; as long as they have a bit of land to go with them and are close enough for the Farmer to drive to work, they see them. Some are worse than the Open House. Some are better. But none are right. They are beginning to lose hope.

"What about that one house?" the Farmer asks. "It has lots of land."

"The one behind the houses?" his Wife asks right back.

He nods.

"No way." An idea hits her. "Wait a minute—why don't we *build* a house? That way we can make it anyway we want." *It can be brick, or stone. And fireplaces, lots of them. It won't have squeaky floors, or drafts, but I'll live,* she decides. *It can have a big kitchen, with a garden right out the back door–for picking.*

"Building a house takes a long time. The man who wants to live in our house won't want to wait that long to move in," the Farmer answers.

"I'll call my sister," his Wife replies. "She has houses to rent. Maybe she'll have one for us to live in while we build our Farm."

And that's just what she does. The next day, bright and early, she calls her sister and asks if she has a place for them to live.

"Why, yes," she says. "One of my tenants is moving out soon. He's just waiting on the people living in his house to move out."

The Farmer's Wife pauses. "What is his name, this tenant waiting on people to move out?"

She says it: the name of the man who is buying the house in the Village.

The Farmer's Wife hangs up the phone, smiling for the first time in weeks.

The Farmer stops mid-stride. "What's up?"

“Everything’s gonna be just fine,” says his Wife. “God’s got his hands in this.”

The Farmer smiles, too. “We’ll find our Farm yet.”

Chapter Six: The Used to be Farm

"How about that one house?" the Farmer asks.

"Which one?" his Wife asks back.

"The one behind all those houses. It's still for sale. It *used* to be a farm—dairy, I think."

"Fine," she snaps. "We'll go look at it."

The Farmer sets up the appointment with the woman who works for the company that sells houses for the next day. It is for right after he gets out of work and since it's on his way, his Wife is going to meet him there.

But she gets there first.

She drives down the long drive, past the houses. People live in those. No one lives in the house that the Farmer wants to see. It is completely empty. The grass is long, and leaves litter the ground because no one has raked them. A swing hangs down from a huge Maple that sits right in front of the house. It moans silently with the wind, either missing the children who were or wishing for the children to come.

She steps past it, past the swing, past the house, past the peering eyes coming from the houses out front. There is a hill behind the house, gently sloping until it meets a creek twisting here and there before snaking out of sight into the woods just beyond it. Her breath catches. It's beautiful.

From where she stands there is nothing, no neighbors, no houses, no noise. Just nothing. Oh, there are trees, plenty of those, and there are birds, many of them—they swoop down to see who she is and why she is there, and frogs ribbiting and twigs snapping, and water gurgling.

And a car door shutting.

The Farmer's Wife takes a deep breath and slowly lets it out. She turns to walk back to the house. Another door shuts—heavier, thicker: The Farmer's truck. Her pace quickens.

The Farmer and the woman who works for the company that sells houses are standing by the house, waiting for his Wife. The woman who works for the company that sells houses is pointing at something on the house.

"...and it has four bedrooms, one for each of the children."

And the big barn that the Farmer wants.

And a pool.

The Farmer's Wife sighs, looking at the house. It isn't brick or stone. And it is new.

"Let's look inside," the woman who works for the company that sells houses says, excitedly.

The Farmer and his Wife follow her. The first room is the living room; it's small, and the ceilings are low, but there are hardwood floors and a big picture window.

The woman who works for the company that sells houses leads them to the kitchen/eating area. The Farmer's Wife swallows hard. No dining room for family dinners. The Farmer looks at her. "It's fine," she says, moving into the next room. A bathroom. Followed by two bedrooms.

They head for the stairs. The Farmer goes first. The stairs creak and groan under his weight. His Wife pauses. Maybe this house *does* have a story to tell.

He turns back. "What?"

She smiles to herself. "Nothing."

Upstairs there are the other two bedrooms and a bath, with a deep soaking tub. The Farmer comes up behind his Wife as she lingers by the door. "Nice bath," he says, knowing her need (yes, need) of no less than two baths per day, sometimes three.

"Um hum," she says, turning. She will not be so easily swayed. Although if she were to admit such things, she would say that the tub hits a mark.

She stops at the top of the stairs, doing a survey. Yes, it can work. It is functional. There will be room for them all. But can she make it into a *Home*? Is she up to the task?

The house in the Village had been charming when they bought it. It had high ceilings and thick woodwork, crown molding and gingerbread trim, leaded-glass windows and a wood-burning stove, just begging to be curled up in front of with a good long book on a frigid winter's eve.

This house has none of those things.

The Farmer leans toward his Wife. "Think of all you can do," he says, reading her mind.

She nods, looking around. She *could* add those things. She could make it their own. Just the week before, she'd gone to a bakery in the Next Village Over. The building was lovely and quant, everything was just so. She'd asked how old the structure was, sure it had to be at least a hundred, maybe two. Their answer was six months. They'd added the charm themselves.

Maybe she can do that, too.

They step back outside, and the Farmer comes up behind his Wife, putting his hands on her shoulders, one on each side. "Well?" he asks. "What do you think?"

"It's perfect," she answers.

Chapter Seven: The Free Sale

No one can believe how fast it has all come together, the chickens most of all. They've barely begun on their packing and ka-blam-oo, it's time to move.

The Farmer calls a family meeting. This time there is no input from others, just instructions for all: Boxes have to be packed, and things have to be given away.

Each gets right to work.

The Farmer looks at the piles and shakes his head. The pile to be packed is twice as big as the one to be given away. "Go through everything again," he says. "We have wayyyyy too much stuff."

The Farmer's Wife sighs and begins again. "Do I *really* need this cookbook?" she asks herself. Deciding she does, it's placed back on the pile to be kept.

The children, each, have their own piles. Theirs, like their mother's, are wayyyy too big.

The Farmer comes back to help. "What is this for?" he asks Jacob, who shrugs, but grabs the thing-a-ma-bob back, gripping it with both hands and arms and legs, besides.

The Farmer moves on to Mikaela's pile. "And this? Do you really need *three* copies of Moby Dick?"

She grips each one, hoping, praying, he does not see the fourth and the fifth.

The Farmer eyes his Wife. She stretches arms and legs and feet over her pile, protecting it from the coming onslaught.

But, come it does.

"What about this? And this? And this?" the Farmer asks, grabbing and yanking things from top and bottom, side and under.

The Farmer's Wife doesn't have hands enough to save it all, try as she might.

The give-away pile grows until it is as tall as the house from which it came. But what to do with it? Who does one give four copies of Moby Dick to?

"We are having a sale," the Farmer announces.

Groans resound. Who wants to sit outside all day in the hot sun—and for what? Money? Time, especially now, is worth far more than money.

"Why not be a blessing to our neighbors?" the Farmer's Wife asks. "Why not have a 'Free' sale?"

And that is just what they do. They take down the pile and place it in the front yard with signs here and there letting people far and wide know that all they see is theirs for the taking.

The Family returns inside to resume their packing in the darkened house— the sun itself can't see through that pile—not even into the highest window!

"Mom! Come Quick!!"

The Farmer's Wife bounds up the stairs, sure that death and Hades awaits her, so shrill was the scream that met her ears.

Hannah is at the window, pointing to the stream of light shining in. The sun has made it! The pile must be shrinking!

And so, it is.

Both look out the window at the mayhem below. Vehicles line the street, each filled to the brim with what's-its and doodads.

"Did you see that?" Mikaela asks, joining them. "Someone just took *two* copies of Moby Dick—I told dad you needed more than one!"

Soon light shines in through all the windows and vehicles become scarcer until there is just one—a horse and buggy.

The Farmer and his Wife join the Family by the road as they struggle to get the wringer-washer into the small space.

"Are you sure you want to give this away?" the Amish Wife asks, looking at the gargantuan machine.

The Farmer's Wife hesitates. She wants that machine, really wants it, and has always imagined herself using it...someday.

The Farmer coughs.

"Oh yes, yes," the Farmer's Wife answers. "It's all yours."

Together they lift it into the back. The horse neighs, objecting. The washer weighs far more than the Family it's used to transporting from here to there.

The Amish Husband pats its head affectionately. In each family there is sacrifice for the sake of the whole. The horse stands taller, strengthened and proud to do its good work.

The Farmer and his Wife turn to go inside, to continue with theirs.

Chapter Eight: Happy Ending/Beginning for Chickens

The neighbors shake their heads the day they move in.

Remember how you were told that the Farm sits behind all those houses? Well it does, and in each one lives a neighbor. And today all of them are watching out their windows. And why are they watching, you might ask? Well, let me tell you. They're watching because behind the truck, being towed by it in fact, is the chicken coop. The Farmer and a few of his friends have managed to get the coop onto a trailer that is just a little bit bigger than the coop itself, which to anyone watching, looks like the chicken coop *is* the trailer. An interesting sight indeed.

The chickens sit and watch the entire thing. They could've sat inside their coop, minding their business, but that's not the way with these birds! They sit on the perch just outside the coop, so they can see their new home with their own eyes.

And so they can make trouble.

The truck stops at the end of the driveway, as is the normal way of things. The chickens, sensing their opportunity, let out a blood curling *cock a doodle doooooooo,* even though the sun has been up for hours and even though not one of them is a rooster.

The neighbors jerk back from their windows in disdain.

The chickens laugh so hard they fall over backwards. What a great joke they've made!

"Where has the neighborhood gone?" each neighbor wonders, letting the curtains drop back to their places.

Where indeed.

The Farmer pulls in the rest of the way, driving behind the house. Working together, each grabbing a corner, they slide the coop off the trailer and onto the long grasses. The Farmer opens the latch. The chickens come out at once, looking here and there, to see if per chance a pesky neighbor lurks with egg in hand. Seeing none, they set about in search of bugs. There are many.

Hannah comes out of the truck and reaches down and picks one up; Chicken Little, a favorite of hers. The chicken sighs contentedly and rests her head against Hannah's chest.

"I guess we're here now," Hannah mumbles.

The chicken answers with a wistful coo.

Chapter Nine: Grandpa's Trees

Now, they move to the Farm on December fourth and miraculously, there's no snow on the ground. And thank goodness for that! If there was, they'd never be able to get Grandpa's trees in.

You see Grandpa, the Farmer's father, had given Hannah and Mikaela an apple tree for their seventh birthdays (Jacob isn't seven yet, so he doesn't have a tree). The Farmer and his Wife planted them in the yard in the Village, but trees can be moved, and that's just what they do. They dig up both trees, wrap their gangly roots in burlap, and drive them to the Farm—to be the very first trees in the orchard.

The Farmer's Wife slides out of the truck and looks around. Where will the orchard be?

The children have lots of suggestions:

"How about in the woods? Trees belong out there." To this the Farmer explains how trees need light and room to grow.

"Down the hill, right next to the creek." To this, the Farmer tells how wet ground is death to a tree.

And…

"I don't care where you put them—as long as I get my apples!" To this the Farmer's Wife rolls her eyes.

After much debating and general bad-idea giving, the Farmer and his Wife walk the yard alone. They didn't see the Farm in the Spring, so they have no idea what areas will be wet—as every Farmer knows (and now as every Farmer's *child* knows) wet ground is death for a tree. They don't want to make the wrong choice.

"A tree can always be moved," the Farmer says, lifting the tree out of the back of the truck, proving it.

His Wife nods. "Let's just get them in the ground up on the hill. We can move them later once we decide where the orchard will be."

"Good idea," the Farmer says, letting her think it was hers.

Now, the trees aren't the only things they bring with them. They have other things, as well—things that *would* never, *could* never be put in the giveaway pile—like that wonderful Rhubarb that grows all summer—They could never leave that behind! It's the exact color needed for Sparkling Pink Drink! As every Farmer and his Wife knows, life is not worth living without it—and no other Rhubarb will make it exactly right.

They also bring the concrete rock they'd made some years back when they'd decided their place in the Village should be named, like all those estates across the pond. It had begun its life as a brick. The Farmer's Wife had poured the concrete into the mold and waited the specified amount of time, but when she'd flipped it over, it puddled into a glob. "Oh, well," she'd said, "I guess you want to be a rock instead." She pressed the letters into place and waited for it to set. Actually, it's a good thing it didn't turn out to be a brick, because if it had, it would've ended up in the fireplace they'd built under the pergola, and fireplaces are not like trees and rocks and rhubarb. They cannot be moved.

Jacob set the rock down between Grandpa's two trees, officially naming their Farm: Eden—the same as their house in the Village; a garden where you walk with God. All gather round and say a prayer, asking God to bless them in this, their new home.

Now that you know about Sparkling Pink Drink, it is a certain thing that you can hardly wait to make some for yourself. To see how it's done, the recipe is in the Appendix at the end.

"PINK DRINK"

Now—a warning—you may be very disappointed in your Sparkling Pink Drink. Maybe it's not quite pink enough (there *is* a reason the Farmer's Wife dug up her special rhubarb—there's nothing like it). Quite simply, not all rhubarb is the same. The kind that grows on the Farm is a deep, rich mahogany pink and grows all the summer long. If yours is not that kind, then please,

please, do not blame us for your vastly inferior Pink Drink. You will simply have to make a trip to the Farm to have the beverage as it was meant to be had.

Chapter Ten: The Mouse House

The Farmer and his Wife lay in bed that first night, exhausted with all the work they'd done. But it *is* done. They are in. They just close their eyes when they hear it: the scurrying, nibbling sound that only a mouse can make.

Here's something you might not know about the Farmer's Wife. She detests mice. She doesn't particularly like cats, either, but she hates mice much, much more, therefore she has vowed that they will always keep a cat on the Farm. But they don't have a cat tonight.

And because of that, they have mice. Lots of mice.

The Farmer, knowing his Wife well, jumps out of bed and sets some traps. To set a trap you need something mice like and there's nothing mice like more than peanut butter. Some people think it's cheese, but they're wrong. Mice love peanut butter.

The Farmer sets the traps loaded to the brim with peanut butter and returns to bed.

Snap. (That's the sound a trap makes when it's caught its mouse.)

The Farmer jumps out of the bed he's just come into to dispose of the mouse and to reset the trap.

Snap. Snap. The Farmer hasn't even made it back in the room this time. Three mice—in the same number of minutes.

The Farmer's Wife lays very still in the bed, pulling the covers up over her head.

Snap. Snap. Snap.

The Farmer doesn't bother coming back to bed. He can't— he's too busy emptying traps and loading them again.

"This is a mouse house!" his Wife whimpers, safely under the covers.

The Farmer, hearing her, comes back in. "Not anymore. This is our Farm now. The mice will have to get used to living outside."

Snap.

Chapter Eleven: The Fifth Day of Christmas

The Snow comes. Yes, *that* particular word *needs* to be capitalized. The Farmer and his Family have moved just in time. Winter will not be held back a second longer. Sometime during the Night of Mice, the first flake falls and is soon met by many more.

Jacob runs into his Parent's room that morning, having slept very well. “Look out the window!”

The Farmer and his Wife groan in unison, pulling the covers over their heads, blocking out the light streaming in. Because Jacob has just pulled back the curtains, as you can plainly see.

"Come on," he says, yanking on their arms. The Farmer relents, getting up. His Wife stays where she is.

"Does this mean it's Christmas?" Jacob asks and then she knows. The snow has come. Christmas equals snow to Jacob and snow equals Christmas. Because for the Farmer and his Family, it does.

Most years it snows all December and *every* year they celebrate Christmas all December, but this year is different. They'd been so busy packing and moving that they didn't realize they'd already missed the first four Days of Christmas.

And Jacob forgot, too. Until the snow.

"Where's my Chocolate?" Jacob spins around to look at his Mother.

"The mice ate it," she answers, pulling the covers back over her head.

"What?" Jacob asks, alarmed.

"In my closet. In the box marked 'Christmas'."

Jacob scrambles toward the stack of boxes lining the inside of the closet walls.

He finds it, his Advent Calendar. That's what he'd meant by 'Chocolate'. He pulls his out and rushes into the living room.

The Farmer's Wife gets up and follows him there, carrying the other four. They each have their own. You've seen these before, haven't you? They're everywhere in November and mostly gone, but half-priced in December, because by then there's no point. You have to begin on the first, because an Advent Calendar is nothing more than a way to count down to Christmas.

Jacob finds the door marked with the number five, because as he knows and you must suspect, it is the fifth day of December. He has it open, its chocolate already in his mouth.

His Mother looks at his calendar. "What about one to four?" she asks.

"You can do that?" His face is stunned.

She nods.

"Are you sure?"

She nods again.

"Really sure?"

She grabs his calendar and pops open the first four doors, taking the chocolates out. She lifts them to her mouth.

"Okay, I believe you," he says, snatching them back.

Hannah comes down the stairs. "Hey! Is that my Chocolate?"

Jacob hands her the one with her name penned on top. She opens door number five, because, as you now know, it is the fifth of December.

"What about one to four?" her Mother asks.

Hannah looks up. "I can do that?"

Her Mother nods.

"Just do it," Jacob says. "Trust me."

The Farmer's Wife smiles.

Chapter Twelve: The Seventh Day of Christmas

The seventh day of Christmas is the best of them all. Always. It doesn't matter if it should fall on a Monday, Tuesday, Wednesday, or Thursday, it's always the same. It is the day of lists. Yes, lists, as in plural. A list is made for each and every thing pertaining to Christmas. A list for gifts wished for and a list for gifts to be made (each kept secret from the other, of course). A list of the Christmas cookies—this list rarely changes, as the Farmer's Wife makes the same ones each year—Christmas biscotti (studded with pistachios and dried cherries for their green and red hues and drizzled in white chocolate), cutouts, and gingery ginger creams. A list for what will be served on Christmas eve, Christmas breakfast, and Christmas Dinner. A list of whom to send the cards to—although truth be told, this list is one they make and then quickly forget. Letter writing takes place often on the Farm, but never around Christmas. That's what visiting's for. Which leads me to the most important list of all: the activities they will participate in. Choices have to be made. They simply can't do *everything*—if they tried, then the most important thing of all would be missed—time with themselves and each other to reflect on what this season really means. With that in mind, it's a yes to the Living Nativity walk. No to the cookie exchange they've been invited to participate in—why would they exchange their lovely cookies away for someone else's obviously inferior varieties? Yes to the gift-making night and yes to Caroling—who would miss that? The calendar is now full, but not too full. There are still plenty of open spaces and dates to be filled with quiet nights spent with each other.

The Farmer's Wife calls the family meeting to order and passes out the lists (except for the secret ones, of course) for everyone's approval.

Each looks down, reading carefully.

"No sledding?" Jacob asks.

"You can't schedule snow," she responds. "When it does, we will be sure to fit it in for you."

He goes back to reading, pacified.

"Might I suggest Prime Rib for dinner on Christmas?" the Farmer asks.

"You may," his Wife answers and crosses out the goose and pens in the Rib.

"Could we do different cookies this year?" Hannah asks.

The room goes silent.

"What do you suggest?" her Mother asks, breaking it.

"I don't know. Something different."

Different? Why make something different if you already have the best?

Hannah looks at her Mother earnestly, who sighs. "I guess we can try. Why don't you go through some of the cookbooks and see if there are any you like."

She smiles and looks down.

"Hey," Mikaela interjects. "I don't see any eggnog on here."

The Farmer's Wife frowns and looks down. How did she forget that? But Mikaela is right. She did. She corrects that immediately by writing it down twice next to the Rib. And again on the bottom, just in case. Everyone knows Christmas wouldn't be Christmas without the Nog!

"Anything else?" The Farmer's Wife asks. All shake their heads. The lists are official.

And because it would be just plain cruel to talk about *the* best Christmas Cookies ever and not share them with you, you can find the recipes in Appendix A. Enjoy!

Chapter Thirteen: The Gifts

The very next day they begin—they must, or it will never be done in time!

First come the gifts, because they take the longest. Why make them then, you ask? Because they're Farmers, that's why. And Farmers make the gifts they give. No store-bought doo-dad will possibly do—not when there are rose-hip jams and Christmas teas; embroidered tea cloths and painted mugs. Not when there is dirt to grow and minds to plan and hands to make.

Now, for the tea towels. The Farmer's Wife has shown them to you, didn't she? No? Then surely she must have told you about them—about how she found a whole stack of those muslin tea towels at the yard sales last summer, knowing they were Christmas-gifts-to-be. And so they are. Twelve in all, in varying shades of crisp white.

Now, she has no idea what this gift will become, you see. The towels hardly know themselves. Such a thing must be discovered.

Getting no inspiration from their crisp whiteness, she rummages through her yarn stash (every true Farmer has a stash of yarn hidden away somewhere) until she finds a deep green wool that is speaking to her. It is the perfect shade for a Christmas tree! And what is a Christmas tree without decorations? Why, it is nothing at all.

"Fetch me my box of buttons," she calls out, and listens as footsteps comply. Whose will they be? Too light a step for Mikaela. Too quick for Hannah.

Jacob sets the box down next to her reverently, wishing to see what she will do with them, knowing as well as you that a button has a million uses.

She opens it, showing big and small, round and shaped, bright and dull, old and new. "Which do you like?" she asks, as Jacob intently inspects each one.

His eyes widen. To be given access to the button box is a great honor. He knows this. His hand hovers. "What are they for?"

The Farmer's Wife smiles proudly. "To decorate a tree," she answers, giving him the information he needs to choose wisely.

His hand that had been about select a red bow moves on in favor of the golden star. He grabs several.

The Farmer's Wife takes his treasures and slips the hunter green yarn through the needle, knotted at one end. She pierces the cloth, setting each button in its place—some for decorations, some for the gifts set under, and one golden star at the top to grace the decorated tree that has appeared on each towel—twelve in all.

The Farmer's Wife hands each to Jacob as it's completed. He in turn places them in the box designated for such things.

"What's next?" he asks eagerly as he peers over the chair where his Mother is perched.

She smiles lightly. "Can you keep a secret?" she asks.

He nods emphatically. Surely, he can.

The Farmer's Wife looks this way and that and leans toward the waiting boy, for such things can only be whispered in the ear.

He leans closer.

"I am making Hannah another Anne doll."

Jacob jumps back, grinning from ear to ear, filled to the brim with the secret information. He knows, as well as you, how much Hannah loves her Anne doll. How she holds her, and sleeps with her each night. How she tells her all her secrets and listens to hers in return. How she is her very best friend in the whole wide world.

See her there, in the corner, lovingly placed. Yes. There she lies, too fragile to be held. Too broken to keep in secrets.

"I am only telling you this very special secret because I need your help."

Jacob nods solemnly. He would and will do anything for Hannah.

His Mother leans close again, whispering in his ear, "I need you to play with Hannah outside. Keep her busy, so I can get this done."

Jacob pulls back and nods once, accepting his mission. He runs off to find Hannah and begin his very good work.

The moment the door is shut behind them, the Farmer's Wife pulls out the pattern she'd used four years before. The paper is crumpled and worn, but perhaps it will make just one more doll. For Hannah, surely it will.

The Farmer's Wife has chosen the softest fabric—just right for midnight snuggles—and lays the pattern on top. At first the paper resists. It has already given so much. It is not willing.

"For Hannah," the Farmer's Wife whispers.

Reluctantly, it sighs. For Hannah.

The Farmer's Wife places and pins and cuts as fast as she can—before the pattern can change its mind.

It seems to, several times, but in the end, mind changed or not, the work has been done. All the pieces have been cut. Now, all that is needed is to sew them together, and the Farmer's Wife can do that herself.

And so she does. The arms and legs are sewn to the body and the body is sewn to the head and all is stuffed with softened down. The orange "carrots" hair is set, each strand of the softest alpaca wool before being braided long and thick down the new Anne's back. A green flannel dress is fitted and made, of the same material and kind as the original Anne.

The very Anne, who is looking on from the corner, smiling softly. She, like you and I, only want what is best for dear Hannah. We only want her to have a friend again.

The doll is just wrapped in tissue and placed in the box when the door flies open, revealing Hannah with Jacob just behind, with frantic eyes searching out his Mother.

The Farmer's Wife smiles at the pair, but most especially at Jacob. "Perfect timing," she says, rising to her feet. "I was just about to make hot chocolate."

Both children scamper to the kitchen, forgetting what they may or may not have seen sticking out of the Christmas Gift Box.

Chapter Fourteen: The Farmer's Gift

The Farmer's gift is simpler, plainer, but just as important. While packing the house from the Village, the Farmer's Wife found a picture of him in his younger years, when he raced those crazy cars around that crazy track. Yes, the Farmer used to race cars—you never knew that? Well, you're being told now. He raced and did quite well, just like his dad before him.

The picture she'd found was a favorite. He was in his racing suit, looking like he so often does; deep, speculative, thinking thoughts that none but himself will ever know. The picture had a frame at one time, had a frame, but had never been hung. You see, it never seemed to go in the house in the Village. That house was pretty and pristine—there was no room for a race car there except out in the garage.

His Wife looks around. There is room for the picture here. Her eyes graze an open wall. A place of honor. It will be one of the few presents she'll be buying this year—a new frame for a new wall and a new life.

Chapter Fifteen: Hannah's Something Different

The Farmer's Wife gathers her supplies—the rolling pin, the bin of cookie cutters, pans, parchment paper, and all the good things that mixed together make up the Cookies. Lastly, she pulls her apron over her head—that means she's all business from this moment on. Sure, she can have fun later. But not now. Not with that apron on.

Hannah steps into the room, a cookbook tucked under her arm. The Farmer's Wife hardly notices. Until she sets that cookbook down on the counter, right in the middle of the pile of supplies.

“What are you doing?” her Mother asks, exasperated. Doesn’t she see the Apron? Doesn’t she know cookie making is serious business?

“I picked out the cookie I want to make,” she says, flipping her book open to a page.

Jacob, who is propped up next to his Mother, gasps. He’d thought Hannah was joking. They did.

Not only is Hannah not joking, she actually begins making her cookies. On this very day.

And she doesn’t do it the way the Farmer’s Wife would. She dumps all the ingredients into a bowl, not separating them at all, and starts mixing them *with her hands!* Can you believe it? The Farmer’s Wife can’t.

She lets out an exasperated sigh and goes back to her own work, keeping her eyes in her own lane, and all good things like that.

The figure leaning against her side shifts.

The Farmer's Wife looks down. Jacob is half-way to Hannah, and more than that, that's where his eyes are fixed.

"What are you doing?" his Mother asks. Doesn't he *see* the *apron*? Doesn't he know cookie making is serious business?

"It looks like fun," he says and moves the rest of the way over to Hannah, who is coloring her dough and shaping it into fruit and other what nots, again, *with her hands!*

Jacob joins her, grabbing some dough and forming something that looks like a car.

"You can't do that," Hannah chides, laughing.

Finally. A voice of reason, her Mother thinks, almost out loud.

Hannah tosses him more dough. "It's got to be bigger—otherwise it'll burn when we bake 'em."

Jacob reforms his car so it's the same size as Hannah's oranges and peaches, apples and pears that line the counter.

The Farmer's Wife moves closer. "Can I try?" she asks, taking off her Apron.

Hannah pushes a pile of dough towards her Mother, who goes to work straight away. She lifts her hand, showing the floppy yellow star that's perched precariously there. "What do you think?"

Hannah smiles. "It's perfect."

"HANNAH'S SOMETHING DIFFERENT"

Chapter Sixteen: The Tree

There are many tree farms by the Farm, and the Farmer and his Family take turns visiting each one. This year they go to a place by the canal. It's run by a man named Tim Buhr.

"Talk about your name picking your profession for you—I'd say Tim Buhr was born to be a Tree Farmer!" the Farmer's wife says, laughing.

They pull up next to the place and get out. She chuckles to herself again as they pass the sign with the namesake posted across it. Tim Buhr. She shakes her head. *That's too much.*

They have trees already cut lining the front yard, but the Farmer and his Family don't want one of those. They want to cut their own.

The Farmer trudges out first, breaking a path in the snow. He has his bow saw in hand, just waiting for someone to announce the right one. But first, a debate.

"This one's the best," Jacob announces, gripping on tightly to a bare patch on the truck of his shabby tree. There are many bare patches and his Mother tells him so. He grips tighter.

Hannah has found her own tree. Hers is tall, almost ten feet, and full and lovely. Her Mother leans towards her. "It's a beautiful tree, but there's no way it will fit. The Farm doesn't have high ceilings like the house in the Village."

Her hand slowly drops.

Mikaela has picked one as well. It's short and fat; as round as it is tall. "This should be the one, I've even named it—Fatbastard!"

Jacob laughs and comes running. "Fatbastard! Fatbastard!"

The Farmer's Wife's eyes flash at Mikaela. "Jacob! That's not a nice word."

The Farmer comes, thinking they've made their choice.

"No," his Wife says, stopping him. "That's not our tree."

"Why not?" Hannah asks. "It's not too tall."

"And there's no bare spots," Jacob adds.

"No."

Mikaela laughs, "Fatbastard! Fatbastard!" The others join her.

"How about this one?" the Farmer asks, pointing to a small tree one over from fatbas...I apologize...Mikaela's tree.

His Wife circles it. It's about the right height and width. There are a few sparse areas, but only on one side—they can put that toward the wall. The Farmer drops to the ground to make sure the trunk is straight.

"Hey, I want to do it," Jacob says, picking the saw up off the ground.

The Farmer sits up. He looks at his Wife. “Is this our tree?”

She nods. It is.

“Come here,” he says to Jacob, moving out of his way.

Jacob drops to the ground, flat on his stomach and starts sawing. The Farmer grips the trunk a foot or so above the saw, steadying it. The tree gently falls to the ground.

“Tim Buhr....” the Farmer’s Wife says and everyone laughs.

The tree is dragged back to the truck and strapped down.

“Remember that year when our tree flew out of the truck?”

The Farmer sighs. He checks the strap, making sure it’s tight.

“You should’ve seen your face!” The Farmer’s Wife makes her face look like his did. “And remember what you said, just before it flew out? ‘There’s no way that thing’s coming outta here.’ Remember? Remember?”

“I remember,” the Farmer answers, tightlipped. “And I also remember you telling that story last year. And the year before that.”

She pats his backside and laughs. He joins her. Just like he will next year.

"The Tree"

Chapter Seventeen: Christmas Eve

The church bells ring in time with the organ—Silent Night. The Farmer's Wife closes her eyes and breathes in and exhales slowly, taking in the icy air. Soaking it all up. Too soon it will be over—a memory inscribed on the heart of Christmases past. But not now. Now it's Christmas. Eve at least. Services have just finished and now the Farmer and his Family need to be scampering home. There are still a few routines to complete before sleepy heads can rest on pillows.

Footsteps stop next to her. She glances over at her son, whose eyes are closed, breathing in, just like she had been, only his tongue is out.

"What are you doing?" she laughs.

His eyes stay closed. "Catching a snowflake," he says around his tongue.

She smiles and closes her eyes again and sticks out her tongue. She's soon rewarded with a soft nothingness melting into a drop. She doesn't know how, but it tastes like peppermint.

"Coming?" asks a restless voice. Someone has waited until the last minute to wrap.

The Farmer's Wife opens her eyes at the same time Jacob does. The moment has passed, but it was there and will be forever: a Christmas memory.

The three of them turn and join the Farmer and Hannah in the warming truck. Christmas music blares out the door as Mikaela yanks it open. It's different than the Silent Night bells—not better, not worse, just different.

The Farmer's Wife sits down and closes her eyes, taking that in, too.

The tires crunch on the snow-laden roads that lead to home. Home. Was there ever such a word on this night of nights?!

The second the truck stops, the three children shove open doors and bound towards the house. They'll go to the living room and wait, knowing full well what's coming next.

The Farmer and his Wife walk slower. Here and there a star peeks through the clouds. They can almost picture one big one, pointing the way. Snow slowly and silently falls. It's a quiet moment. A holy moment.

The Farmer's Wife takes the Farmer's hand. "Ready for this?"

He chuckles. Restful and quiet is the last things the next twenty-four hours will be. But it will be good.

Together they walk to the house and go to the tree where the Christmas Eve gifts are waiting. Now about the gifts. They're always the same: Christmas pajamas. A pair for each.

And yet there the children all sit, waiting expectantly, like they have no idea what those rectangular boxes hold.

They wait patiently as the hot chocolate is made. It's the same recipe, same marshmallows, same whipped cream that's made on every other cold day. The difference is the mugs. Tonight and only tonight, it's poured into Grammy's Irish coffee mugs, remembering days and years ago when the Farmer's Wife looked over the edge of the counter as her Grammy poured the frothy chocolate, warm and good, into those very same mugs.

The Farmer's Wife sips hers contentedly as the Farmer hands out the boxes, one to each, keeping the one with his namesake tucked beside him. Hannah rips hers open: a fuzzy pair of footies spills out onto the floor. She scoops it up and holds its warm softness to her chest. "Oh! Thank you!"

Jacob and the Farmer are next; because as the Farmer knows and Jacob suspects, they have matching boxes for matching pairs: both with red and green stripped bottoms and t-shirt tops. Mikaela's are button down top and bottoms, bright red and silky. The Farmer's Wife sets down her empty mug to open hers. It's a nightgown; plaid flannel, soft and lush, with eyelet trim around the sleeves and neck. It's a nightgown fit for a Farmer's wife. She smiles, stroking the fabric lightly.

The Farmer leans towards her. "Do you like it?"

Most gifts they make or buy together. This nightgown is one of the few things he bought on his own. She squeezes his hand. "I love it."

Chapter Eighteen: Christmas Morning

Now from what's been told, most kids are up bright and early on Christmas morning. That has never been the case with these kids! The Farmer and his Wife always wake up an hour or more before the sun... and wait. At seven his Wife can't take it anymore.

Neither can the Farmer.

"Quit your pacing and go get the kids."

She screeches to a halt mid-stride and bolts up the stairs, turning on lights as she goes. "Get up! Get up! It's Christmas!!!"

The greeting is met with groans. "What time is it?" one asks.

"Time to get up," their Mother answers.

No responses are made from little heads tucked in little beds.

Christmas music wafts up the stairs; the Farmer turned it on in anticipation. (He's as bad as his Wife.)

The Farmer's Wife brings out the big guns. "Well...if you don't want to open presents..."

That gets them going.

Six feet rush past and down the stairs and the Farmer's Wife turns, to follow them.

She places herself next to the tree as the official hander-outer-of-gifts. Her hands graze the box with the new Anne in it. She pauses and lets it pass. That needs to wait until the end. Instead, she grabs a box for Jacob and hands it to him. The paper flies off in heaps and is followed by squeals of delight. A beebee gun. He's wanted one for forever so long.

Mikaela is next and hers is predictably a book—this one an older edition of Little

Women. It is set safely aside for further investigation.

The Farmer's Wife pushes a gift towards the Farmer, who ignores it. He grabs one for Hannah instead. She rips it open, discovering scraps of paper and other crafty odds and ends that she's sure to turn into something beautiful.

The gift is nudged toward the Farmer once more. This time he opens it. He smiles looking down at himself enframed. His Wife reaches behind herself for the hammer and nail she'd stashed by the tree. "I know just the spot for that."

Standing, she leads him to the open place on the wall. He pauses and smiles and takes the hammer and nail and pounds it in its place. Carefully, gently, he places the frame in its home, tapping it here and there, making sure it's level.

They all stand back in admiration. It is made to go there.

The Farmer is the first to speak. "Alright. Let's finish with those presents."

And so they do. Mikaela gets several more books and bright green mittens. Jacob gets a target for his gun and a pouch for his "ammo". The Farmer's Wife gets a book or two herself and a box of chocolates from a special spot in Kentucky—a nod to a memory from a trip long past.

Hannah's box lays unopened until the very end. "What's that one?" she asks leaning towards it. "It says my name."

"Go on, open it."

She slides her finger under the paper, saving it to add to her stash. The box pops open once released from it's paper bindings, showing the new Anne, looking up at us all.

Hannah stares, wide-eyed—either in horror or happiness. It's hard to tell.

"It's a new doll," her Mother says, reaching over. "I couldn't fix the old one."

Hannah flinches, dropping the 'new' Anne. "You didn't throw her out, did you?"

"Of course not," her Mother reassures her. "She's where she's always been—safely on your bed. This is a new Anne. A *fixed* Anne."

And then her Mother saw what she should've known all along. Hannah wouldn't want a new Anne any more than she wanted a new house. Even if it didn't work, the familiar is preferred.

Tears well in her Mother's eyes and she picks the doll off the floor.

Hannah yanks it back. "It's not Anne," she clarifies. "But she could be her new friend."

Her Mother nods. "Yes, she can be that."

Hannah smiles, looking softly down at her new doll. She has room in her heart for both the old and the new.

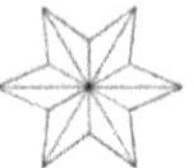

Chapter Nineteen: Christmas Dinner

The Farmer and his Wife host Christmas; that started years ago in the Village, because they were the ones with the big dining room and even though the dining room is gone now, the tradition has been set. They just must (somehow) make room for two aunts, two uncles, a Grandma, a Grandpa, six cousins, and themselves: a full house to be sure.

A sit-down dinner is out of the question—no room for tables! So, a buffet it is. There's Prime Rib (as requested by the Farmer) and potatoes a couple different ways, and vegetables, and the squashes, and of course the Farmer's Wife's famous stuffed mushrooms, crab cakes, and sweet and spicy pepper dip. They're required fare. Aunt Willow brings the salad and Aunt Emily the veggies in their various shapes and forms. Mema (aka Grandma) is responsible for at least one of the potato types and two of the squashes. And the Farmer's Wife makes the dessert—a simple chocolate mousse. And the Nog, of course the Nog. Can't forget about that! Again.

All in all, a veritable feast, resulting in more than one adult sprawled out on a couch or chair, top button of their pants undone, stomach shifted to the side in a most undignified but completely acceptable Christmas position. When else do you eat so much you quite literally burst?

"Come outside with me," one child asks. A groan is their only answer. The children have yet to learn to eat to excess on Christmas. They are still able to run and play.

Good for them.

The ladies begin the dishes. Now I know what you're thinking—how unfair of you—here the ladies do all the cooking and the dishes as well? The answer to that is simple. The Farmer's Wife does the cooking because she enjoys the cooking and she does the dishes because they need doing, and where else can you get a room full of your favorite women working around a task and talking comfortably with each other? So, because of that, the dishes are enjoyable as well, and the part of Christmas the Farmer's Wife looks forward to most of all.

The men-folk may sprawl, and the women may work, but I will leave it to you to decide for yourself who is enjoying the holiday more. Just look at the two groups—one is laughing heartily, while the other is asleep. Enough said.

And because it has thus been decided that the kitchen is the far pleasanter place, that is where we will now draw near.

The Farmer's Wife is doing the washing while Mema dries. Aunt Willow and Emily gather and wipe and put the dishes away.

"I noticed the picture of the Farmer," Mema says as she hands a dish off to Aunt Emily to be placed in the cupboard.

"Yes," the Farmer's Wife answers. "It looks just right, doesn't it?"

All agree.

"And I saw Hannah playing with her new Anne doll."

"She's naming her Ann without an 'e' so as not to confuse her with the original."

"That seems very practical."

On and on the talks go, dipping, raising, in soft cantors, covering all the events of the day. Aunt Willow has received a composter—something she's been sorely needing and Aunt Emily a tea pot—a need in its own right.

Mema is most excited about the sleds; one for each grandchild that she and Papa (aka Grandpa) found and restored, which will be perfectly suited for sledding down a particular hill on their property. She has been praying for the snow to come and come and given her direct link to the Divine, the rest of the women look out the window fearfully. No one wants another blizzard.

One lazy flake flitters to the ground and they all laugh. Some more nervously than others.

The husbands rouse themselves and announce the evening finished. Children are gathered and stuffed into coats and hats and mittens.

The Farmer and his Wife follow all outside, waving and hugging and well wishing.

More flakes have joined the first, falling not so gently as the cars speed away, trying to beat the storm.

And beat it they do, but not before the ground is coated with white and white and more white.

It looks like tomorrow'll be a day for sledding after all.

Chapter Twenty: Snow

The Farmer's Wife glares out the window. Leave it to Mema. She prayed so hard that the snow would come—and come it did. And now it won't leave!

The ground is covered with the stuff! And the branches on the trees and the bushes here and there—all of it—are covered in a literal blanket of snow.

"You could pray, too," the youngest reminds her. "Pray that it all goes away."

She looks at the calendar and sighs. She has a feeling God will say no. It is January, after all. No, they are stuck. But not everyone minds, the children in particular.

The Farmer's Wife bows her head and folds her hands and walks to the window to check—just in case—when a voice calls out behind her, asking if it's still there.

She turns and sees Jacob, mittens and hat on. His face eager, like he's hoping she'll say yes, crazy child that he is.

She sighs. "It is."

In a flash he's gone. Out the door to play in the stuff. Can you believe it? He actually plays with it. Making men. Throwing it here and there. The Farmer has shoveled some into a heap; that's where Jacob is now—on top of that massive pile.

The Farmer's Wife turns away from the window at the sudden sound. "Not you, too?"

Hannah is bundled thickly: hat, gloves, jacket. "Yeah. It looks like fun."

"Fun?! Are you crazy? That *stuff* makes it so nothing can grow."

"I thought the cold did that," Hannah answers smartly.

"Just you go and ask your chickens how much they like it."

Hannah frowns, looking out the back door. It is true. The chickens have signed a proclamation stating they flatly refuse to leave their coup until the white stuff is gone. Therefore, Hannah must visit and hold them each in their abode. Daily. Otherwise, no eggs.

Hannah sighs, but continues towards the door.

“You’re still going?” her Mother asks, incredulous.

“Spring will be here soon,” Hannah says and with that she is gone.

The Farmer’s Wife goes back to looking out her window.

The Farmer’s pile is soon molded into rooms with tunnels between. The slide that has been formed on one side is made faster and faster each time Hannah or Jacob goes down. Their cheeks and noses are rosy and their breath shines. Squeals of delight filter inside.

Is it fun? the Farmer’s Wife wonders.

A picture fills her mind; of white piles made into bakeries and icicle lollipops. Of troops of rosy-cheeked kids all in a heap. Of never wanting winter to end.

Can it be true? Could snow be...*fun*?

Seems there is only one way to find out.

The Farmer's Wife slides into her winter pants and jacket, hat and mittens—you know the ones she knitted last winter from the wool she bought online? The peach and white ones? Yes. Those.

The cold, crisp air fills her lungs. Refreshing, but not in a good way. Maybe she's remembered wrong. Maybe it was sand...not snow. She turns to go back inside where she belongs.

Whack.

She slowly turns and faces the child who has another ball of packed fluff in his hand, all ready to launch. "Jacob I wouldn't do that if I were—"

Whack.

The melting mush slices into her face before sliding to the ground with a thump.

The smile on Jacob's face freezes, then disappears. He turns and runs, but not fast enough.

Whack.

"Hah! I got you!" The Farmer's Wife scoops up more and flings it, this time at Hannah.

"Mom! I wasn't playing."

"Y'ar now!" She pelts two more at her.

Hannah shakes her head, trying to free it from the melting goo.

Whack.

She spins around. Jacob's hit her from the front this time.

"Jacob!" she squeals, scooping up whatever her hands can findand what they can find is one for Jacob and one for her Mother.

"I'm so ..so..so..cold," comes a little voice.

His Mother pulls him in for a hug. "Come on inside. I'll make us some hot chocolate."

Hannah drops her weapons and heads for the door, already shedding her layers.

Apparently, she wants some, too.

Chapter Twenty-One: Rest

In the North, where the Farm is, the dirt sleeps all winter. It's tucked in under a thick blanket of snow. No planting can be done, and no planting means no harvesting, and no harvesting means no crisp green beans to have with supper and no peaches for pie. But it does mean rest, and for more than just the dirt. The Farmer and his Wife, and all the children rest, too. They're forced to. The frozen dirt just won't give no matter how hard they try.

But their minds? They never get to rest—not when there's a Farm to start. Plans must be made. Beginning with the Garden.

Everyone knows you cannot have a proper Farm without a garden, no matter what type of Farm it may be. The Farm that Used to Be Here was a dairy farm, but no garden plot could be found (the farmers who lived here before must not have known about the rule concerning gardens and Farms and that you *must* have one). Because of that, there was only one thing that could be done. A new garden plot must be chosen. And for so important a matter, each member of the family was required to attend.

All put on boots and hats, scarfs and mittens and trudge outside. The bitter wind howls as it whips scarves here and there, slapping their faces in the process. More than one child complains.

The Farmer's Wife turns to look at said child. "Do you really want to miss this momentous event? Do you want to have to tell your future children, my grandchildren, that you could've been part of the Laying of the Land, but you didn't, because it was *too cold*?"

A blank stare is her answer.

She turns to face the Farmer. “Well? What do you think?”

He scans the field, the hill, the creek. “Seems like a great place for deer.”

She looks as well. He’s right. It’s a deer’s playground. Now don’t misunderstand, they don’t mind sharing the crops with those living around and with themselves, but sometimes deer can be a bit greedy. They don’t like to leave any for a Farmer and his Wife, let alone their children.

“Might be best to put things as close to the house as possible,” the Farmer adds. “Maybe that’ll keep them out of the cabbages.”

There’s a flat piece of land that lies just to the East of the house, right past the swell, and that is where the Farmer’s eyes rest. It’s bound to be soupy and wet in the Spring—no place for a fruit tree or two or twenty to grow, but a garden? It will be just right for that. You see, The Farmer and his Wife garden with raised beds, so soupy soil doesn’t matter.

The Farmer must feel the same as you and me, because he begins to pace out a smallish garden.

His Wife laughs and follows behind, making a path in the snow at least twice the size of his.

He frowns. "Are you serious? How many veggies do you think we need?"

"Lots of them. Lots and lots." Her face gets distant as plans form. She turns to go back to the house, where her stash of graph paper lays hidden, where no Farmer knows where to look.

The Farmer sighs, knowing his Wife all too well. This garden was fixing to be ginormous.

The children turn to follow. Grandpa's trees see them and wave. They wave back before heading inside to see their Mother's drawings over a cup of hot cocoa.

"GRANDPA'S TREE"

Chapter Twenty-Two: Garden Plans

Now that the spot is picked, it's time for the Planning. Oh! how the Farmer's Wife loves a good plan. She has lots of them. Some to run, some to sit, some to build, some to tear down. Everything has its plan and place and this garden will be no different.

A loud sigh comes from behind her. She turns. The Farmer has seen the graph paper. She chuckles and gets back to work.

So he can start his.

There will be patches for berries: straw and rasp. Blue and Huckle. And one for tomatoes. And peppers. Oh, and the herb garden—it will be divine! Each patch is placed on the paper in exactly the place they will be in the soil.

The Farmer leans over his Wife. "What's that?" His finger points to a spot on the paper.

"A cottage. For writing."

"I thought we were doing a garden."

"Of course we are!" she exclaims. Doesn't he know that the only good and perfect place for a Farmer's Wife to have a writing cottage is right in the middle of the Farm? And what can be more in the middle than the garden? She tells him so.

He stands at full height. Arms crossed.

She sighs and goes back to work, getting a new sheet of paper. The raised beds shrink. So does the cottage. There will barely be room for a desk, let alone everything else! (And by everything else she means her record player and all that goes with it, a table for tea, a couch to sit upon, and shelves upon shelves of books.)

Another grumble.

She turns. "What now?"

His finger points to a spot on the paper very close to where her cottage sits, beautiful in all her carbon gloriousness.

She pulls out a third piece of paper.

Her pencil skims the paper, right where the cottage should go.

"No."

She turns. Horrified. Did he just say *No*?

"The actual garden needs to come first. The Farm. Remember?"

This time it is her who folds her arms across her chest—for a whole ten minutes she sits there. *No cottage? Who ever heard of such a thing?* She grumbles. Heavily.

After her ten minutes are up, she sighs and pulls out a fourth piece of paper. Raised beds are drawn. Seven four by four, two four by eight and one four by ten; all making a perfect rectangle—all around an open space in the middle. Open and waiting.

Her pencil touches the paper.

"Melanie."

“A pergola?” she asks. With a picnic table under. For writing. “A pergola, like we had at the house in the village, with clusters and clusters of grapey-grapes?”

“A pergola,” the Farmer concedes. “But no cottages.”

“Alright.”

“What’s going in-between all the raised beds?”

“Grass, of course,” she answers. What else?

“Who’s going to mow that?”

“Me,” she lies.

The Farmer laughs. “I guess it’s a good thing we kept that old push mower.”

Yes. The push mower that only he can start? Yes. It’s a very good thing.

The Farmer’s Wife pulls out another sheet of graph paper. The Farmer stops. “What’s that for?”

“For drawing out the West garden.”

He points to the other drawing. “Then what’s that?”

She smiles. “The East garden.”

A loud laugh follows. “No cottages.”

“No cottages,” she answers.

For now.

Chapter Twenty-Three: Shrove Tuesday

Spring brings with it more than Robins and tulips, planting and plans. At the Farm. they celebrate Easter, and by that, I mean *really* celebrate it. It begins some forty days before when they make pancakes. Yes, pancakes.

The Farmer's Wife flips another onto a plate. "I don't think I can do it," whimpers one.

"Toughen up," she laughs and slaps on another. A big one.

"What does this have to do with Easter?" another asks and their Mother shrugs. She has no idea. Well, that's not entirely true. She knows it has something to do with cleaning out your cabinets before you start to fast. And since some people fast over Lent, sometime, somewhere, people started making a mess of pancakes the night before.

She just knows she likes to eat pancakes.

And here's how she does it: You have to start the night before, mixing equal amounts of wheat flour (freshly ground is best) and yogurt into a bowl. That sets out until it's nice and bubbly—overnight at least. To that you add an egg or two, a teaspoon of soda and half as much salt and a tablespoon or so of melted butter. And with that, you will have the lightest, fluffiest pancakes around.

The Farmer's Wife has made a triple batch, just for the occasion.

They have chocolate chip pancakes and blueberry pancakes, cinnamon and spice pancakes with sizzling apples, pumpkin pancakes and yes, even plain ones. But no matter the kind, all get topped with warm, golden maple syrup—straight from the tree. They'll have no darkened sugar-water from corn served here, let me tell you, not when there's a maple tree left standing within a hundred miles.

Groans sound from around the table. Buttons are let loose.

"How about some more?" she asks.

Chairs scrape back. There's a mutiny, and this one's begun by the Farmer himself.

"Please. No more."

She laughs and puts her spatula down. Let the fast begin.

Chapter Twenty-Four: The Thankfulness Walk

Now, about this fasting business. Some do it and some don't. It's not so much a rule at the Farm as it is an option if one should choose it.

"Whatcha giving up?" the Neighbor From Across The Road asks the Farmer's Wife as she makes her way to the mailbox to place a letter she's written.

She pauses, unsure. Not unsure if she's giving up something or not, she plans to do that—fasting in some way or another has always served her as a sort of reminder–whenever she craved whatever it was she'd "given up" she would offer up thanks to God, instead.

But what will it be this year? What will she miss on a daily basis? Do you have any ideas? Because she's stumped. And that's just what she tells the Neighbor.

The Neighbor From Across The Road shakes her head. "You better get picking, quick. Lent's already started!"

"I know, I know," the Farmer's Wife moans. "What are you giving up?" she asks, hoping for inspiration.

"Coffee," she answers. "That or chocolate."

The Farmer's Wife nods. Both would be difficult, and certainly something she would miss every day.

The Farmer's Wife places the letter and makes her way back, still undecided. While it is true she has coffee each day, that is only in the Morning-time. She needs the kind that will be an all-day-long Reminder.

A gentle tug comes at her sleeve. Hannah slips her hand around her Mother's. "Wanna go for a walk?"

She does, so they do. The yard is coming to life. Birds swoop and breezes puff. *Thank you God for this Farm and this little girl who lives in it.*

That little girl bends down to pick an early flower—a crocus—and places it in her Mother's hand before bounding for the house.

Thank you, God for this flower.

The Farmer's Wife sighs, feeling full to the brim. A smile comes to her soul right before it lands on her face. Maybe instead of giving up a thing, she can add a thing, a thing that makes her thank God all day long.

Nothing makes her thank God more than being outside, right there in the middle of His Creation.

With the flower tucked safely in her hand she rounds the yard, finishing for the first time her new routine: the daily thankfulness walk.

Chapter Twenty-Five: The Christian Seder

To *really* celebrate Easter, it must been given its full week, and that the Farmer and his Family do, beginning on Palm Sunday, continuing with the Seder on Maundy Thursday (more on that in a bit), a somber church service on Good Friday night after it's gotten dark and dreary, and then, finally, the celebration on Easter Morning.

Now for the Seder, it goes like this. A leg of lamb is roasted with a bit of garlic, olive oil, and rosemary, and some potatoes are treated the same. There's roasted roots (carrots), and a bit of unleavened bread to go with the wine, but that's just the food. A Christian Seder is so much more than that. It is a remembrance of the Passover, yes, but it is also a celebration of Jesus, who with His Life and Death allowed us, His children, to be "Passed Over" from Death to Life.

Some years the Farmer and his Family celebrate amongst themselves, and sometimes they include others. This year is the later type, because they're setting it up at their Church. This happened because the Farmer's Wife (and her Mother, who wrote the service) got to thinking that something so very precious should be something that's shared.

And so they do.

Tables are set with the finest linens, because this is a time to bring out your very best. On each one is placed a platter with small crystal bowls; one for the salt water (Israelite's tears) and one for horseradish (their bitter labor). One for parsley (life), and a basket for the unleavened bread and a carafe for the wine and/or grape juice. In the very center is a candlestick, one. For the Light of the World.

There's an extra napkin on each plate, to catch all the drops of wine as each plague is recited aloud.

The Farmer's Wife glances at each table, making sure everything is just so before going to the church kitchen, apron on. There's work to be done. Lamb and potatoes to roast, and carrots, too. Mikaela's already in there, busy placing the bread into the baskets. Mema's checking on the roasts and stirring the carrots.

One by one the families come and settle in. The Farmer's Wife pulls out the lamb and covers it with foil to rest and joins the others who are already sitting.

And so, the Service begins.

Wine is poured and drunk, Verses are recited and pondered. Children speak their parts, as do the Men and Women. All participate. A Hymn is sung.

It's time to break bread together.

The Farmer's Wife and Mema, Mikaela and others from tables here and there go to the kitchen to plate up the lamb, potatoes, and veggies. Plate after plate is carried out and set before man, woman, and child until each has their fill.

And the Service continues.

Verses are spoken and recited, as the Passover Remembrance shifts into something far more beautiful—the Lord's Supper.

Eyes close as tears slide down cheeks. Oh, what He has done! For you and for me! It is too much, too much loveliness. All we can do is fall silent in awe and gratitude.

The service concludes and all look, one to another and see glistened eyes all around. The Farmer's Wife is certain. The precious gift she has shared has been received and is sure to be repeated. She has no doubt each present will continue with this tradition with their families from this night on.

After all, why would you keep such a thing to yourself?

Slowly, quiet conversations begin. A gentle peace surrounds all. Every worry, every nagging doubt, every consuming sin. All of it. All are gone. All are nailed to the Cross.

And all that is left is sweet love and gratitude, for the Lord, and for each other.

Chapter Twenty-Six: A Bright New Day

Church begins at sunrise on Easter Morn. For a Farmer, this is nothing new. The sun and the Farmer are old friends, you see, and meeting daily is something of a custom.

The children, however, feel differently.

"Are you serious?" comes a muffled voice from under the piles of blankets. Those blankets quiver as their Master gains a tighter hold, surely knowing what's coming next.

Their Master is not disappointed.

With one giant pull, blankets and the like are ripped from the bed and the singing begins. "Rise and shine and give..."

A pillow flies through the air and lands on the head of the Farmer's Wife. Yes! On Her head! Cutting off her song for all who were enjoying the hearing of it.

She moves along to the next room, stopping only briefly to gather up blankets and sheets and pillow, in case the occupant of the bed should decide to bury herself once again.

The next room is dark, silent. Even breaths are rare. Has he heard the ruckus from his sister? Small hands are curled around the top blanket, gripping tightly.

He's heard.

The Farmer's Wife pauses. Waiting. A small head peaks out from under the covers. Their eyes meet. The blankets are quickly replaced, but it is too late. He's been seen. He sighs in forfeit, for he knows the rules. Once seen, one has no choice but to comply with the Waker's every command.

There is no need to go to the third child's room, for she is already up, working on the morning breakfast- it will be pancakes once again!

Finally. Forty days is far too long to go without a good pancake.

Slowly the rest come in and fill their plates, ignoring the dark shining in through the windows. Good coffee is ground and percolated and graciously accepted, by even the smallest of hands.

A moment of quiet and contemplation is enjoyed before the ciaos begins. And it does begin. Hats and tights are applied, ties are tied and knickers knicked. Together they head out in the dark and gloom, waiting for the bright new day.

And it is a bright new day, for it is Easter Morn!

Others nod in their direction as they enter the church.

Their children look at the Farmer's with understanding. The Farmer's Wife smiles to herself. Surely, they were awoken with song as well.

They find their places in the pew.

The organ begins. With its sound the first splash of light hits the stained glass and falls lightly on those gathered here. The Day has begun.

The Farmer's Wife closes her eyes and her heart swells with the now familiar act of thankfulness, practiced each day of the last forty.

Thank you, Lord, for this day. For this moment.

The organ hits its highest notes—a crescendo. *But most of all, thank you for showing me who You are and who I am and how much I need you each and every day. Thank you for dying for me and rising for me, so when I die, I will rise and be with you forever. Amen.*

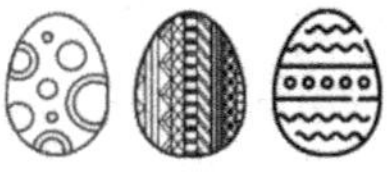

Chapter Twenty-Seven: The Hunt

After church, there is breakfast at Aunt Willow's, but before all of that, there is the Egg Hunt. Now, a thing or two about the Hunt.

There are several eggs hidden here and there of various colors and filled to the brim with goodies and things delightful to both the hearts and stomachs of children and adults alike. But the children are not searching for these. Oh, they will pick one up if they happen to stumble upon it, but it is not the object of their affection, not the reason for this Hunt. No, each child is searching for the Golden Egg.

This egg, larger than the others, is not adored for its yellowed metallic hue, although that does aide in its grandeur. No, this egg is the object of the Hunt because it contains a five-dollar bill, and finding it results in being known as: "The-One-Who-Has-Found-the-Golden-Egg" until the title is up for grabs again on Easter of next year. Yes. The stakes are high.

Each child leans forward, waiting for the signal that the Hunt has begun.

"Go!" Aunt Willow announces, and all obey. Each scrambles away, eyes on the ground, in the sky, and on each other, in case one of their fellow competitors shows by eye or gesture some indication or secret knowledge of said eggs where-abouts.

Jason, The-One-Who-Has-Found-The-Golden-Egg, has held that title for the last two years. He, naturally, gains the most attention. Especially so by Jacob and Eliott. They're desperate for a win.

Elijah streams past, a glint in his eye that goes unnoticed by all but Hannah, who stops her search and turns to follow.

He stoops down. The gutter drain is hanging lower of late. Could it be weighed down by a Golden Egg?

Whoops and Hollers come from the back yard. Elijah straightens, head tilted to the side. He scrambles to his feet and begins filling his sack with the lesser eggs. Now that the Golden Egg has been found, there will be a mad dash for the rest. He knows this.

Hannah bends down and reaches into the abandoned drain. She has it! The Golden EGG!!

All come from the back to congratulate her.

And now, before you feel too bad for Elijah for having missed his chance, look at him there, where he sits under that tree, hand and face coated in chocolate, from a bag weighted down with egg upon egg. Rest assured. He has no regrets.

Chapter Twenty-Eight: The Other Farm

A garden must have plants, just as an orchard must have trees, otherwise it's all just dirt alongside a mown field. And in order to have plants and trees the catalogs must be consulted. For the trees, that matter is simple and already decided. You see, during Autumn (only those who truly love the Fall can call it by its true name: Autumn) the Farmer and his Family traveled to a Neighboring Farm where many fruit trees grow. These Farmers were kind enough to let them sample their goods and choose which trees were right for their Farm To Be. Gala and

Pristine for the apples, as well as a Spitzenberg, a Sweet Sixteen or two, and a Blushing Maiden. For the peaches they went with the famous Haven. The cherries? All tart. They're sweet enough here on the Farm. They don't need any of that nonsense from their cherries, let me tell you. And plums are the faithful Stanley. Twenty-four in all, including the two they already have—the Red Delicious and Empire apple trees from Grandpa. And mulberries–seven in all. Three for the birds and four for them. All of these trees, and the berries for the West Garden, came from their Amish neighbors, the very ones who supplied such sumptuous varieties to their friends from the Neighboring Farm.

Now the West garden is not a garden at all, but a patch; a patch of berries. Straw and rasp, blue and the hip of the rose; all will be included in this fabulous spot of dirt, flanked by the most amazing rhubarb on earth, loving brought from the House in the Village, to find its place of rest here, in order to faithfully supply them with rhubarb all summer long for their refreshingly lovely pink drink, as mentioned prior.

Now, for the garden itself, selections must be made. Some plants will be purchased—like that pesky celery that no one and I mean no one (truly, no one) can grow from seed, but most will begin the way God intended—straight from the seed itself. Now, there are seeds and there are seeds, and the seeds of the likes and kinds the Farmer's Wife wants to plant come from catalogues.

These catalogues came in the mail right after Christmas. There are so many seeds to choose from! Does she try a new sweet pepper—or stick with the tried and true pimento (perfectly sweet and spicy, just right for her sweet and sassy sauce). It's tempting. And that's just peppers. There's also onions, tomatoes, and squashes to consider, not to mention the cantaloupe! Pumpkins and beans, peas and radishes, cabbage and carrots. Beets and beets and beets.

She glances down at her paper. How will their garden hold half that much? And what if she's wrong? What if the soil here won't grow a single thing? The dirt at the House in the Village is good; rich and brown. You see, the Village is right by a Lake, which gives the dirt all the worms it needs. The fisherman would dump out their extras and the worms would make their way to the Village and the dirt was the better for it. Here, at the Farm, there is no lake, no fisherman, no worms.

"Gala and Pristine for the apples, as well as a Spitzenberg, a Sweet Sixteen or two, and a Blushing Maiden"

"Maybe we should get our veggies from another farm," the Farmer's Wife says to the Farmer. "Until we can be sure."

"Do what you think is best," the Farmer answers.

She looks at the catalogues. She looks at her garden plans. Better to be safe then end up with no veggies this summer. A summer with no creamed onions is not worth having.

She places her order for the staples, things she knows will grow no matter what the conditions: Kentucky Wonder beans, Amish Paste tomatoes, Pimento peppers. Detroit beets. Winter Luxury pumpkins.

That's it.

She grabs the envelope and places the stamp. Right before it's stuffed, she adds one more: Paris Market carrots. What if the Other Farm doesn't have those? With a deep sigh she seals the envelope and looks up the number for the Other Farm. It's a road over and set next to a grand old home, one of the oldest around. The original owners have passed away a year or so ago and their grandchildren came back to run the place the best they could. They have shares to sell. It will be just the thing to get them through this, their first year.

The next day she places the call.

"Hello," the Farmer's Wife says. "We bought a Farm the next road over. We're new to this farming business and would like, if you don't mind, to buy a share in yours, just until we get ours going."

"Of course," says the Woman on the Phone. "That will be $$$."

The Farmer's Wife gasps. So much? Their vegetables must be really good. "Let me call you back," she says and places the phone on the receiver.

Her next call is to the Farmer's mother. "Do you by chance want to go in on a share of vegetables with me from the Other Farm?" she asks after they've exchanged pleasantries.

"Buy vegetables?" she asks. "I thought you were bringing a Farm back to life right where you are."

"Yes," the Farmer's Wife concedes. "But there is no lake here, which means no fisherman, which means no worms."

"Well," the Farmer's mother answers. "Where does the Other Farm get their worms from?"

The Farmer's Wife sighs. She doesn't know. She only knows that they absolutely will not have any at the Farm, so far from the lake.

"Yes, I will go in on a share with you," the Farmer's mother says. "I like my veggies."

The Farmer's Wife lets out another sigh, this one in relief. The summer is saved. They will have creamed onions after all.

Chapter Twenty-Nine: Sleeping Trees and Garden Boxes

Now that they've been assured of a good harvest, the Farmer's Wife can go back to creating their own. The Farmer and She take their weekly walk around the yard, jotting down notes as they go.

"There's a Robin," the Farmer's Wife points out before logging it.

They stop their walk and listen. There's dripping all around—from the eves of the house and the barn—from the tips of the tops of the trees. The ground beneath their feet doesn't crunch anymore. Instead, they sink into its softness.

"Spring's here," the Farmer says, seeing the same as his Wife.

She takes a deep breath in. The crispness is gone; replaced by puffs of freshness—found only when Spring makes its presence of-fic-ial.

There are flowers now, real flowers. Not just the tiny crocuses who show up in the earliest of springs, when Winter still has a very real chance of coming-a-calling.

Spring is here. She jots that next to the picture of the Robin.

"The trees need to go in."

She nods. Trees need to be planted when they're still asleep, and soon they'll all be awake. "Today?" she asks.

The Farmer sinks his shovel into the dirt. It goes in four, maybe five inches before it stops. "Tomorrow or the next," he answers. "The ground's still a bit frozen."

His Wife glances toward the barn, where the trees lie sleeping. They'd picked them up from their Amish neighbors a week ago, being very careful and quiet as they set them in the barn, covering them with hay, lulling them back to sleep. "Soon," she'd whispered. Soon. Like a lullaby.

But what if they woke up before the ground did? What would they do then? How could they have juicy peach pies and tart cherry jam? Not to mention the mulberries! What would the birds do without their mulberries?!

They'd move on to the tomatoes, that's what.

"We have to get then in soon!" the Farmer's Wife cries. "I can't live without my tomatoes!"

"Yes. But not yet."

Her hands wring, anxiously.

"Why don't we start on the boxes today?" the Farmer adds. "The snow's gone; it would be just the right kind of day to do it."

Yes, that will work.

Just the day before, the Farmer's friend had dropped off a stack of cedar boards, cut from old telephone poles that had needed replacing. You see he's a Lineman—which is a fancy way of saying he works on those electric lines scattered along the roadsides all the country over. Being a Lineman, he naturally bought a saw to make use of those old poles. He was nice enough to cut them into boards for the Farmer and his Wife to use in their garden.

They'd stacked them in the barn—those boards—on the outside they're faded and grey—but not on the inside—on the inside they're new and full of life and so excited to become the next thing they're to be; in this case they're to be the garden of the Farmer and his Wife.

The Farmer and his Wife head to the barn where their Saw is. Now about the Saw. It had been Papa's Saw and Poppy's before that. It had built shelves and cabinets, dollhouses and cradles—all the lovelies that graced the Farmer's Wife's childhood and her mother's before her. And now it would make their garden.

The boards start out twelve feet long, which makes cutting them into four-foot boards rather simple. Once that is done, they move onto the four eight-foot boards and the two ten. Once cut, the Farmer's Wife holds the boards together as the Farmer screws them tight, binding them for all eternity, or at least until they rot back into the dirt from which they have come.

Now, because the Farmer and his Wife don't like useless work, they apply a layer of weed cloth on the bottom of each box. This cloth makes it so they can place the new garden directly on the lawn, with no fear of weeds poking through, pretending to be vegetables.

There are seven small boxes, two medium, and one large, and now that they're made, they're carried out to the plot of land that will be their home—the very one the Farmer and his Family paced out through the snow.

The boxes are quite light and can be moved and shifted until they're placed exactly right. The Farmer's Wife turns here and there, surveying, as the Farmer gently kicks a box now and again, squaring them up.

There are twenty-four inches between each box—just enough for a lawnmower to pass through—and enough for a kneeling gardener to weed and to pick. In the middle is open grass- where the pergola (cottage-in-the-future) will go.

"Is it good?" the Farmer asks.

She spins one more time and nods. It's just right.

Now, because they have no idea about the dirt on the Farm, the Farmer and his Wife have decided to fill the boxes with potting soil. Bags and Bags and Bags of potting soil.

And Bags.

And Bags.

"Mikaela!" her Mother calls. "Hannah!" They will need many hands working if they are to get this done.

Two girls stream out of the house, jackets on. The Farmer points to the pile of bags. Mikaela's eyes widen. "What do we need all that for?"

Their Mother points to the garden, a great distance from where the bags now sit.

"Are you kidding me?" Mikaela asks.

Their Mother grabs a bag and hoists it over her shoulder to show her she is not in any way shape or form 'kidding' her.

The Farmer strides past, a bag on each shoulder.

And so, the work gets done. The boxes fill and the new dirt smiles up at the sun, missing it from being in those bags ever so long.

The sun smiles back and waves its good-bye. It's been a good day of good work.

The Farmer stops beside his Wife, leaning on his shovel. The end sinks into the soft soil. "Looks like tomorrow'll be a good day for planting those trees."

His Wife smiles. So it is.

Chapter Thirty: The Mulberry Farm

There's a soft, rolling hill that runs alongside the Farmhouse, gently rising until it peaks and falls, landing, finally, at the creek. It's here, where the hill begins, that the Farmer and his Wife decide to place their orchard.

Grandpa's trees are settled in first, as the gentle watchmen they are; Mikaela's in the front corner, with Hannah's just behind. The other apples fill in the first two rows. The cherries are next, followed by the plums. Finally, the peaches are in the back corner, at the highest point—they need the drainage more than the rest.

Twenty-four in all.

"Where do you want these?" the Farmer asks, nudging his foot towards the eight mulberry trees.

Now. About the mulberries. Growing up, the Farmer's Wife lived by a park, and in that park was one giant mulberry tree. Each year, for Fourth of July, Mema and Papa, Willow, Emily, and Herself, would pick bushels of the sweet, hand-staining fruit and make pies. In fact, they still go to that same park and pick those same berries each year. The Farmer's Wife has sworn a pledge each year—from age three to thirty (something), that if she were ever to have a Farm of her own, she would have one of those majestic trees.

So, they bought eight.

The thing about mulberries is that you really only need one. One produces lots and lots of berries—that tree in the park gives many, many pies to many, many families each Fourth of July. And Mulberry trees grow very fast.

So why buy eight you might ask?

Just in case.

Just in case one doesn't make it, they will still have seven mulberry trees and if two don't make it, they will still have six mulberry trees and so on and so forth.

The Farmer's Wife picks up the bunch of eight saplings and carries them to the very front of the yard, where the ground is a bit moist. Another thing about mulberry trees is that they can grow in wet dirt. So that's where they put them. All eight.

The next morning the Farmer and his Wife go for their walk around the yard. Much has changed—leaves are beginning to bud on the trees—they're walking up! They planted their trees just in time!

The Farmer frowns, pointing to a tree. "What do those leaves look like to you?"

His Wife peers closer. A tiny triple pointed leaf smiles up at her. "Mulberry?" she asks.

The Farmer nods. “And this one?” He plucks another leaf from a neighboring tree; a sprawling, fully mature tree.

“Mulberry,” she whispers, looking up at the three huge trees sprawled out in front of them. She groans.

They will have mulberries coming out their ears.

"He Was Born A Farmer"

Chapter Thirty-One: Mother's Day

"What will you be wanting for Mother's Day this year?" the Farmer asks, giving himself a good two weeks before the Day itself to construct whatever it is he's been instructed to make.

The Farmer's Wife considers this. There is no shortage of things she would have him make, but most of them he already has, or plans to. No, this year will be different.

"I'd like to meet the Farm," she answers, thinking of the mulberries she's just been introduced to. Maybe the Farm had even more to tell.

The Farmer nods and begins making the arrangements.

Two weeks later, the blessed day arrives and the Farmer's Wife dons a pair of the Farmer's thickest rubber boots.

The Farmer takes her by the hand and leads the way to the creek and the board he's laid across it, his hand gently on her back in case she needs it.

Paths have been carved, two weeks-worth, leading this way and that.

The Farmer heads left, knowing that holds the most surprises.

His Wife trods along and stops. "Is that..?" she steps closer to investigate. It is indeed. An entire patch of wild black raspberries. She squeals with delight. They are her very fav-or-ite!

The Farmer smiles and leads on.

His Wife stops again, this time leaning low. A white petal has caught her eye. "Wild strawberries!" she exclaims and is quick to make the introductions. There are also wild onions and chives, an ancient willow swaying in the breeze and no end to the wild roses.

The Farmer stops along the path and waits. Before them lies a steep hill, just the kind for sledding.

He leans towards his wife. “Over the river and through the woods...”

Her eyes gleam, picturing years and days of sledding parties and hot chocolate sipping.

And black raspberry pies. And wild strawberry tea.

The Farmer leads back. This time up and over a felled tree. Hannah is perched there, legs dangling down, just grazing the creek below.

The Farmer’s Wife sets herself down beside her while the Farmer heads back to the house.

The leaves whisper their secrets and the creek bubbles along. And legs swing back and forth. Two sets.

Minutes pass. An hour.

Hannah gets to her feet. “Coming?” she asks.

Her Mother shakes her head. “Give me a minute.”

Hannah goes the way of the Farmer.

The Farmer’s Wife breathes in deep and full, letting it out slowly.

“It has been so very nice to meet you,” she whispers as she gazes around.

She sits another minute and goes her way.

Chapter Thirty-Two: Home Schooling

Some children go to school in buildings, and some use their computers. The children on the Farm do their schooling at home—they have for forever so long. Mikaela's almost done—this is her last year—and then she'll be off to college to do who knows what (even she isn't sure). Hannah and Jacob are a bit younger, so they have years and years left.

Oh! You've never met a homeschooling family? Well then. You came to the right place. Let's take a closer look so you can acquaint yourselves with the process.

See Hannah? She's right there, on the sofa. Yes, I know, she's still in her pajamas.

That's the official homeschooling uniform. But what is she *doing* while perched there ever so comfy on the couch in her p.js? Yes. She's drawing. And look how alive she is while she's doing it!

You see, the Farmer's Wife knows her very well. She knows she hates to read. But reading's important, so she's gone at it from a different angle. Every time Hannah reads a book, her Mother has her illustrate it, however she will.

"Just close your eyes," her Mother says, and Hannah obeys. "Do you see the story in your mind?"

Hannah nods.

"Now draw it."

And Hannah does. She grabs the paper and scrambles to get the picture down before it fades from mind and page.

Now Hannah reads all the time.

Let's move on to Jacob. I'm sure you'll find him outside, drinking in the sunshine. Now, let me see, where did that boy go? He's always here and there, never in the same spot. He's an explorer that one. Oh. Yes. There he is. Down by the creek. See him there? Yes. He's squatting down—that's why it was so hard to find him. Do you see that in his hand? And that book on the ground? Yes. That's a microscope—the kind that fits in your hand. And that book? That's his nature journal. He's just found another bug to log. That kid and his bugs, I tell you! It's all well and good until he tries to bring them in the house. That's where his Mother has drawn a line.

Have you seen it when he's tried? And how his Mother jumps up and runs! Oh, it's a hoot! If you haven't, you simply must. It's a scene you won't soon forget.

Now, I don't want you getting the wrong idea. His Mother doesn't mind. Not really. Not when he loves it so. And not when it covers science and writing and art all in one!

On to Mikaela. Let's go find her. It shouldn't be hard. Mikaela tends to stay put. And put is in her room, where all her books are. Yes. Just as I thought. There she is. She's got a thick book spread wide across her face. I can't quite make out the title. Can you? No matter. At least, since it's thick, we can be assured it's not a play. Hopefully, this means she's moved on from her Shakespeare stage. Thank goodness for that! It is so very hard to answer someone in sonnets.

Let me see, where did their Teacher go? Ah. There she is, in her garden, weeding again. It must be a Thursday.

See how calm and happy and contented she looks? How they *all* look?

Do you hear those birds chirping? And feel the breeze and the sun and the *wild*?

It's truly a wonderful way to craft a life!

Chapter Thirty-Three: They Tried to Kill Hannah!

Not only does Hannah not like to Read, she doesn't much like to Write, either. But seeing as both need to be done, her Mother has come up with a way around that, too.

And it goes like this:

"Hannah, I have an idea," her Mother says one night.

Hannah freezes. She's been the victim of her Mother's ideas before.

"Let's go out to eat, and you can take notes. You can jot down what the restaurant looks like, what you order, how the food was, stuff like that. And then, you can post your review online."

Hannah's face brightens.

"Let's go tonight," her Mother says, while she's still excited. And so they do.

Hannah gets to pick the spot.

The building is brick, she jots down in her notebook. *With windows all down the front.*

The Farmer and his Wife and Hannah make their way inside.

They seat us right away, in a booth by the fireplace.

They're handed menus.

The menu has lots to pick from, but I choose the chicken fingers—they're my favorite.

The Farmer and his Wife and Hannah wait.

They gave me a worksheet to draw on, and some crayons, which is very thoughtful.

The dinners arrive and a platter of chicken fingers is placed in front of Hannah.

"Now, I want you look at them," her Mother says. "So you can do a good job describing everything, not just how they taste."

Hannah flips them over, examining each closely. Her hands freeze. "What's this?" she asks, pulling out a long metal shard from one of her chicken fingers.

Her Mother takes it, eyes wide. The Farmer slides the plate away from his Daughter.

They tried to kill me. Seriously.

The Farmer's Wife calls the waiter over and hands him the metal. His eyes go wide, too. More waiters come. And a manager. All apologize for trying to kill Hannah. They investigate the matter thoroughly. They come back and say the fryer basket broke apart, and some must have gone into Hannah's chicken. They say how very sorry they are, again and again.

"We forgive you for trying to kill Hannah," the Farmer's Wife says. "But please, replace the basket so no other children find metal in their chicken!”

They promise they will.

Hannah grabs her notebook and the Farmer and his Wife take her to eat somewhere else.

Chapter Thirty-Four: The Standoff

It's a warm spring day, the day a neighbor came walking down the long drive towards the Farm. The Farmer and his Wife are out, placing the plants in the boxes.

"Hello!" the Neighbor Up Front calls while still a way off.

The Farmer and his Wife get to their feet and make their way to the smiling woman with a basket of goodies in her hands.

"Welcome to the neighborhood!" she says as they get closer. She is an older woman, small, with a warm smile that covers each part of her face.

She points to the house directly in front of the Farm and says that that house is hers and had been her mother's before her. Her sisters and their families live in the other houses and all are happy the Farmer and his Family are there.

"Who lives in that house?" the Farmer's Wife asks, pointing to a lone brick house, unkempt and crumbling.

The Neighbor Up Front crosses herself and replies, "You'll want to stay away from *that* house."

The Farmer's Wife waits for more, but that is all she is willing or able to say.

"You're doing so much here!" the Neighbor Up Front interjects, changing the subject.

The Farmer smiles and points out the gardens and the orchard. They walk her to where the clothesline will be.

She laughs. "Oh, you'll regret that! Between the mulberries and the birds your clothes will be ruined!"

The Farmer's Wife looks at the Farmer and the Farmer looks at her. No wind-whipped clothes? No bringing the outdoors in every time you slip into freshly laundered sheets? No crinkly towels ready to suck the water off your just-bathed body? What will they do?

The Farmer laughs nervously. "I think we'll risk the birds."

The Neighbor Up Front smiles knowingly and turns to leave.

The Farmer's Wife looks at all the mulberry trees, their blackened berries juicy and ripe. She turns to the Farmer. "Do you think she's right?"

He starts, then stops, seeing the same thing as his Wife. A bird, a robin in fact, flies overhead, swooping down just over their heads, landing itself on one of the large mulberry trees that line the barn, just thirty feet from where the clothesline is to go.

It smiles at them.

The Farmer frowns.

“We had a clothesline in the village,” his Wife sputters.

“We did,” the Farmer agrees.

“And birds…”

“Yes.” He eyes her.

“…and berries…”

“But not mulberries.”

The bird’s smile grows leaps and bounds as he plots and plans.

The Farmer’s Wife whimpers. But begin they must and so they do. This very day.

The clothesline itself is easy to make. It’s just two posts placed in the ground a good distance apart. On those posts boards are placed, one on each, with cords, as many as you please, connecting the posts—that’s where the clothes go.

The Farmer sets each in place and nods towards his Wife, who is watching safely from a window.

She walks out, carrying a basket of freshly-laundered sheets and blankets—old ones. This will be a trial run.

The birds are silent. Watching. Waiting.

She takes a sheet, white as the clouds overhead, and clips it onto the cord closest to herself. She prays it will stay that way.

Before long, all the sheets are placed.

She stands back and waits. The robin watches her from a tree, head tipped to the side. It is waiting, too.

It's a standoff.

But, unfortunately for the Farmer's Wife, it is one the bird will win. The Farm isn't going to run itself, certainly not if one stands around all day looking at birds. The Farmer's Wife goes back into the house.

Every now and again she stops by a window. Oh, how the birds try! They dive, they swirl, they loop-de-loop. With each spectacle her heart sinks. How can one have a Farm with no clothesline? It isn't possible.

Hours later the Farmer's Wife goes outside to assess the damage. Crisp white sheets and blankets billowing in the wind wave to her.

She waves back, moving closer. *Is it possible?*

She inspects each one, burying her head into the closest, breathing in the smell of the wild, caught somehow; miraculously, in this cloth hung out in it.

This spotlessly clean cloth. The birds missed.

The Farmer comes up behind his Wife. “How bad is it?”

She turns, joyously. “We may have a ridiculous number of mulberry trees…but we also have ridiculously blind birds!”

The Farmer laughs and his Wife joins him.

Chapter Thirty-Five: The Singing Tree

In the front of the Farm there is a tree, an ancient, sprawling maple, whose branches and limbs overshadow the house and most of the front yard. And hanging from the tree is a swing.

The Farmer's Wife hasn't been on it. There isn't time for swinging, not when there is a Farm to bring back to life.

She was thinking just that very thought when a sound floated to her ears—soft, then fading, soft, then fading.

The Farmer's Wife peeks around the corner of the house, where the sound is coming from.

The swing—there is someone on it, and they are swinging. And they are singing.

The Farmer's Wife's eyes lock not with the singer, but with a Neighbor. Not the one from Up Front, or Across the Road, but One Over. She is weeding, just like the Farmer's Wife had been doing. Only hers isn't a veggie-patch—it's a flower garden—with a bench and a memorial stone in the middle. She smiles at the Farmer's Wife; a tear sliding down her face. Together they look at the swing and the small girl standing on it, singing her heart out. Singing her sorrow. Singing her pain. Her hair whips in the wind, covering her face, covering her own tears for the house and the friends she's left behind.

The Farmer's Wife turns, not because she has work to do, there is always that, but because such a moment is precious, and private.

She learns one thing. There's always time for swinging.

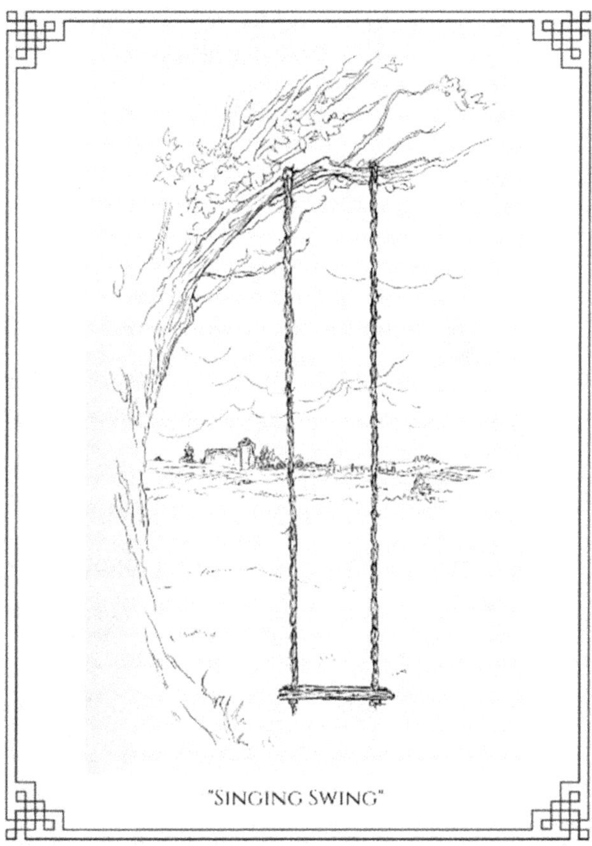

"Singing Swing"

Chapter Thirty-Six: Waffle Wednesday

At the Farm, visitors come and go all the time, but most especially on Wednesdays, because that's the day the Farmer's Wife makes Waffles. It's hard to say which came first, the Waffles or the visitors, or if they both came together. More than likely it's the later. What else is there to make for a singing, squirming, running, playing group of visitors, especially if the day in question is a Wednesday?

The Farmer's Wife can think of nothing.

So, Waffles it is. Big thick ones; rich ones, full of cream and butter and eggs. Just right for topping. Because, as you must surely know, a Waffle is nothing at all without being topped.

Today there are thirteen in all (People. Not Waffles). Of course there's the Farmer's Wife, Mikaela, Hannah and Jacob, besides them, there's a Bessie, a Ruth, a Lila, a(nother) Hannah, an Isaac, an Amanda, an Alexis, an Alayna, and finally, a Collin. Whew! That's a lot!

Hannah and Lila prepare a performance while the Farmer's Wife, Bessie, and Amanda make the Waffles and toppings. Today there will be mountains of whipped cream, mounds of farm-fresh butter, freshly plucked strawberries, and, of course, the Syrup, and by Syrup, I mean Maple. I believe you've already been told how they feel about their Syrup here on the Farm, and how vastly inferior varieties will not be permitted, least of all spoken of.

Plates are laid out, platters filled, and lastly, finally, the children are called in.

They must've been waiting by the door! Look how fast they flood through! See that one—he's already grabbed a plate without washing his hands first! For shame!

Each are sent to wash up and all return and form a proper line. But first. They pray.

Lord God,

Thank you so very much for bringing our friends here together today. And thank you for strawberries. And whipped cream. Let it nourish our bodies.

In Jesus name we pray,

-Amen

A plate is handed to each, as well as a fork and a cup of milk. The first makes her way to the line-up. She looks at the platter of waffles, just waiting to be topped. She looks at her already too-filled hands.

A conundrum.

She's passed by one who has wisely set down his milk in order to have his hands free. He stabs a waffle or three and places them on his plate and moves along. The frozen girl claims his wisdom, as do all the others, and soon all plates are filled and waffles Topped.

Feeling pleasantly full, all head outside to see Hannah and Lila perform. I recommend not missing it. They put on quite a show.

Chapter Thirty-Seven: The Favorite

"Do you love me?" a child asks.

His mother stops her working and looks down. "You know I do."

"The most?" He looks up at her sweetly.

"No."

His face falls. "You mean I'm not your favorite?"

His mother pats him gently on the head. "You're my favorite little boy, but I only have *one* favorite."

He frowns. That wasn't the answer he wanted.

He's so sad about it, in fact, that he tells his sister. "Mom says I'm not her favorite."

He pauses for a second and adds, “And neither are you.”

Well, that gets her going. For the second time in five minutes the Farmer’s Wife is stopped in her work by the same question.

And the same answer is given.

Both children now go to Mikaela, assuming she is the Favorite.

“Of course she is,” one grumbles. “She came first.”

Mikaela agrees. Being a lover of evidence over theories, she goes to consult the woman in question.

But she never gets a chance to ask. The Farmer has just come in, and his Wife is busy filling his mug with fresh, hot coffee before he goes back out-of-doors to finish his work.

Before he turns to leave, his wife kisses him lightly on the cheek. “*You’re* my very favorite,” she says softly.

He smiles down at her before going on his way, like this is something she often says and does. It probably is.

Mikaela smiles, too, and returns to her brother and sister to tell them the good news: that all is right with the world.

"THE FARMER AND HIS WIFE"

Chapter Thirty-Eight: Date Night

Dates of all kinds and sorts happen at the Farm and off it. Sometimes these dates include many and sometimes just one. In fact, the only thing needed for a date is time spent. Meaningful time.

In the case of the singular date, the Farmer's Wife may spend an evening (or morning) (or afternoon) sitting away in a coffee shop, writing all her heart has in it.

At other times, the date is with herself and one of the children. Taking each to their own special places, maybe playing a board game or three over a cup of tea of the bubble variety.

And the Farmer takes dates, too. Only his are his kind, done his way. They may start with a hey let's go back in the woods and cut up that tree. Or a how about a family drive?

Whichever it is, time is spent together and that is always a good thing.

There are, of course, dates between the Farmer and his Wife. These take place on a weekly basis. Sometimes out of the house, in the way of a restaurant meal followed by a trip to a store of some sort to plan out the Next Thing For The Farm. And some dates take place at the Farm itself.

If that is the case, the children are fed and sent on their way.

"How come we only get spaghetti, and you get *that*?" one asks, seeing the crab and cheese and veggies, all lined up.

The Farmer's Wife simply smiles, and they know. Not only are they having spaghetti for dinner, that dinner will be followed by an early bedtime.

Some grumbling ensues, but not much. Nothing that can't be ignored.

The Farmer's Wife goes back to making the **Seafood Pie**, a favorite of the Farmer.

And this is how it's made:

Peppers are chopped fine, of the red, yellow, and orange sweet varieties—enough to make up **a cup**. These are placed in a cast iron skillet, along with a **heaping spoonful of reserved bacon fat**. Because, you see, whenever the Farmer's Wife makes bacon, and that's fairly often, she pours the leftover fat into a crock, and sets that crock in the fridge, so they may have the flavor of the bacon on the odd days when the bacon itself is absent.

A **sweet onion** is also chopped fine, equaling **a half cup**. This is placed with the peppers, along with **three minced cloves of garlic**. The pan is set to heat and its contents stirred until it sizzles a bit and smells like Heaven. A **half cup good white wine** (the Farmer's Wife likes wine of the

Riesling variety) is poured over all and cooked a bit.

The pan is removed from the heat and half its contents spooned out and placed in a bowl and set aside. The pan is placed back on the heat and **two tablespoons flour** are added and stirred in. The mixture will look a bit Globish, but no worries. It will all work out just fine. Once the flour has had its time to cook, **an eight-ounce bottle of clam juice** is added and stirred in and left to bubble. **A half cup heavy cream** is poured in, as well as a **quarter cup freshly grated parmesan cheese.** This is stirred until all is smooth—except for the lumps from the peppers and onions, of course! **A quarter teaspoon salt** and **pepper** are stirred in, as well as a **pinch of red pepper and one of Old Bay**.

The pan is taken off the heat and set aside to cool. To the bowl with the reserved peppers/onions/garlic/wine/baconfat (yes, it's one word), a **cup of pulverized butter**

and garlic croutons is added. It is stirred well and set aside. This will be the Topping.

A pie shell is constructed. You may have your own recipe, and that's good for you. Feel free to use it. Or you may buy one ready-made. Many do. But, if you want to venture out a bit, the Farmer's Wife is including her recipe here:

Take **four and a half ounces flour (one cup)** and add to it a **half teaspoon salt**. Cut a **half cup butter** into small pieces, being careful not to touch the butter with your hands as you're cutting. Place that in with the flour and the salt, and using your pastry blender, food processor, or two forks, cut in the butter until it's the size of split peas. To this add two to three tablespoons very cold water. Start with the two first. If it comes together, leave it at that. If not, add the third.

And by coming together, I mean get your hands in there (Unless you're using a food processor. Don't put your hands in that.) and form it into a ball. Once it is, flour your workspace and roll out your dough until it's big enough to fit into a nine-inch pie pan. Place it in the pan and set it aside.

Now, back to that Filling. It should've had sufficient time to cool while you were making your crust, if not, wait until it is. Once it is, **one pound lump crab meat** is added (Or whatever seafood combination you like, provided it's cooked. The Farmer and his Wife like their crab, so that's what they go with.) The entire concoction is spooned into the waiting pie shell and smoothed out on top.

The crumb Topping is sprinkled over it all and baked in a four-hundred-degree oven for forty-five minutes, or until bubbly.

Please, whatever you do, let it set a bit before cutting. It may be tempting to dig right in there but trust me you'll regret it. Your lovely pie will resemble more of a dip. A delicious dip, but still, a dip.

The Farmer's Wife likes to pass that time by making things a bit fancy by setting out the wine glasses and linen napkins.

It's a table set just for two, for some time well spent.

Chapter Thirty-Nine: A Solution

The chickens had been placed right behind the house when the Farmer and his Wife moved in and they greatly appreciated their spot. There were bugs aplenty—and it was good for the Family as well. They didn't have to trek miles through deep snow to feed and water and gather eggs. And the chickens themselves were safer, close by the house. Many a fox had watched from the woods, hoping against hope that the Farmer and his Wife would place the chickens out with them, but they did not.

Now that the Garden and Orchard have found their home, it's time for the chickens to find theirs. The Farmer and his Wife want the yard behind the house for themselves.

On their walk, the Farmer and his Wife discuss locations. The Fox listen, tongues hanging, fingers crossed.

"In the orchard?" his Wife asks. The chickens can eat all the bugs that could hurt the trees.

The Farmer considers that. His eyes meet with a Fox, lingering just behind the brush. "No," he answers. "That's too close to the woods."

His Wife nods. That is true.

"By the garden?"

He shakes his head. "Too close to the backyard."

His Wife sighs. Is there no place for their chickens but the woods? The Fox, sensing her thoughts, pull out fork and knife.

The Farmer turns. "How about by the barn, under the Mulberry trees?"

The Farmer's Wife gasps. Brilliant! Birds love mulberries—and their chickens were technically birds, so they could eat their fill and keep the Robins from contaminating the laundry!

Because, you see, it had been reported to her that each Robin who called the Farm home had made appointments at the Ophth-alm-ologist. They are more determined than ever to get her sheets.

And now, they won't be able to. The chickens will get to those mulberries first.

It's a win/win for everyone!

"Let's move them today!" she exclaims.

The fox sigh, resigned to wait for a better opportunity.

Chapter Forty: Imposters and Old Friends

The plants are growing nicely now and not just the ones the Farmer's Wife wants. In fact, there are many growing she does not want at all.

She shakes her head as she makes note of those...those...Imposters!

"What's that?" the Farmer asks, pointing at the yellow and green on the page glaring up at him.

"Weeds," she answers. "They're everywhere."

The Farmer nods as his eyes scan the horizon. He knows. His beloved grass is filled with them. They've taken over.

"Hmph," his Wife huffs. "They're not getting my garden!"

That very day she sets about her good work.

Now, the thing about weeds is that they are very smart. They lay down all still like when you come near, only to pop back up again when you turn. And when they do, they stick their tongues out at you.

It's true, I swear it.

And not just that. They change how they look to make themselves seem to be the plant you're trying to grow. Tomato weeds look just like tomato plants and pepper weeds look just like pepper plants.

But there is one way to know for sure—the real plant pulls up easy. Not a weed. A weed you have to yank and yank. I am sorry to say that many a good plant had to perish for this vital information to be gained.

The Farmer's Wife sits down next to a box and gives a plant a gentle tug. It fights back with all it has. She smiles to herself.

Ha! Got ya! She pulls and pulls and the weed finally comes, but, as is usually the case, leaving a part of its root behind, making sure it can come back another day.

Her hand reaches down to grasp the next imposter, but it grazes something slimy instead. She looks down. “Why, hello!” she cries. “It is so very good to see you here!”

The worm looks up at the Farmer’s Wife’s greeting and smiles. And it isn’t just the one. It appears all her friends have come with her! It is practically a worm party!

Tears glisten in the Farmer’s Wife’s eyes. The worms have found their way here from the Lake. They will have a Farm after all!

Chapter Forty-One: No Farmer

The Farmer who runs the Farm the Next Road Over calls on the Telephone. “Our vegetables are ready. You may come get them now.”

The Farmer’s Wife squeals with delight. Oh, just imagine all the creamed onions she will make!

She places a call to the Farmer’s mother. “Our vegetables are ready!” she exclaims.

“Yes, I know. You brought me a bunch of Kale just yesterday.”

The Farmer’s Wife pauses. “Oh! Not *my* vegetables—the vegetables from the Farm the Next Road Over. They’re ready for us to pick up.”

"But don't you have lots of tomatoes and onions, kale and cucumbers?"

The Farmer's Wife looks at the jars of pickles and the stacks of pans filled to the brim with roasted tomatoes, just the kind she uses for Sauce.

"Well, yes," she answers.

"More than you can possibly use?"

It is true. The garden has given so much. There are beans and celery to pick and itty-bitty pumpkins and squashes to be watched. There is zucchini for bread and zucchini for roasting and zucchini for stuffing and finally zucchini for giving away. And lettuce. And onions. And peppers. Lots of peppers.

The Farmer's Wife sighs. What will she do with more?

"I'm coming," says the Farmer's mother. "And we will go pick up our vegetables. We can always freeze them."

Together, they go to the lovely Farm. There are hordes of people picking up, just as they are.

The Farmer's Wife *does* need garlic. That is something you need to plant in the Fall, and during the Fall, they didn't have a garden to plant in.

Yes. She will get lots of garlic. Sweet *and* sassy—that's what her sauce will be!

They take their place in line. They watch as each leave, bag in hand. One bag. The Farmer's Wife looks at the Farmer's mother. She looks right back at her. One bag? For $$$?

The Farmer's mother leans toward her. "Maybe they didn't get the same share we did."

The Farmer's Wife nods. Maybe.

The line moves. It is their turn. They are handed a bag. One. "You may have three of this kind of vegetable and two of this and..."

The Farmer's mother looks at his Wife and she looks right back at her. Someone in the line grumbles. They want their turn.

The Farmer's Wife's eyes rest on the garlic, large and plump, lying on the wagon towards the back of the barn. At least her sauce will still be sassy.

She picks up a bulb.

"No! Not that one!" the Farmer from the Farm the Next Road Over exclaims. "That is what we are taking to market."

The Farmer's Wife looks at the wagon. It's loaded with vegetables, every kind you can imagine. Tomatoes and peppers, onions and Kale, Broccoli and Cauliflower, beans and potatoes, itty-bitty radishes and colossal rutabagas. Much more and much nicer than the ones lining the table at the front of the barn.

"Here," she says, handing the Farmer's Wife a bulb, half the size of the first. "You can take this one, but you'll have to put back the beans."

Her eyes zero in on the Farmer's mother who has just taken three beans and placed them in their bag.

The Farmer's Wife takes a deep breath and says loud enough for all those still in the line to hear, "You are no Farmer! A

Farmer gives their very best. A Farmer shares what they have."

The Farmer's mother smiles as she places the beans back on the table next to their bag. "I know just a Farmer like that!"

Together they go back to the Farm where they fill many bags for the Farmer's mother to take home and enjoy.

Chapter Forty-Two: A Cheese Break

At quarter to three on each and every sunny day the Farmer's Wife gathers her gingham cloth and heads out of doors. All stop and watch her progress.

They wonder, as surely you are, what cheese it will be today.

Let's take a look and see.

She sets down the cloth under the Maple tree, smoothing it out until it is a proper square again. The Basket is set in the middle, to keep it (that pesky cloth, always trying to escape) from billowing away.

Oh! It's so hard to be patient! It's like she *knows* we're waiting...

Okay. There she goes. She's opening the Basket.

She rummages through it a bit, bringing out its treasures one by one. Oh, good. The platter is first, and on it, the cheese. It looks like she's gone with a dollop of mascarpone today, drizzled with golden honey. Next to that is just-picked berries of the wild rasp variety. And finally, because a proper cheese platter must come in threes, there sits a freshly baked pie, just as it is.

Cups are placed next and filled to the brim with sparkling pink drink. (What else?!)

The cloth is set for three, being a weekday, with the Farmer being away at Work and all. That must mean the other plates are for Hannah and Jacob.

Mikaela prefers her cheese inside, at a proper table.

Jacob is the first to arrive. He takes his seat next to his Mother. The two are soon joined by Hannah, who grabs a berry or four and sets them on her plate.

“Are these from this morning?” she asks, having been one of the berry-pickers to make the trek into the woods. She scratches at the mosquito bite on her arm, to prove it.

Her mother answers in the affirmative before popping a few into her own mouth. It has been quite the year for wild berries. They’ve gathered nearly eight quarts from just the back patch alone.

Pictures of jams and cordials fill the Farmer’s Wife’s mind as she itches absently at the bites on her hand. Yes, it’s been a wonderful year!

Hannah reaches for a slice of pie just as Mikaela sits. Those present go still.

Has the Cheese break worked a miracle?

The Farmer’s Wife quickly reaches in the basket for her emergency cup and plate.

Mikaela is handed one of each before she can notice. A slice of pie and smear of cheese is placed just as quickly.

But it’s too late. She’s seen them. The swarming bees and hovering ladyflies.

They like cheese break, as well.

After a moment of indecision, she settles in. The cheese is just good enough that she has decided to stay.

The Farmer's Wife closes her eyes and breathes in deep, saying a quiet prayer of thanks. Thanks for the breeze that carries the scent of the wild, thankful for the berries that carry its taste, and for her daughters and her son, whose lives are now enriched by both.

"A FRESHLY BAKED PIE, JUST AS IT IS."

Chapter Forty-Three: Something Else

Now about chickens. There are several on the Farm, and those enjoy each day—having their fill of mulberries and bugs.

"Would you like to try something else?" the Farmer's Wife says to the Farmer one day. A chicken passes by, dropping a fresh egg as she goes on her way.

The Farmer bends to retrieve it. "Something else?"

"Yes," she continues. "Maybe a cow, or a goat."

The Farmer frowns. "We don't have enough grazing room for a cow and I've never been partial to goats."

"How about a guinea hen, then?" she asks, pulling out the book on guineas she has tucked under her arm.

The Farmer studies the page.

"Here, look," she says, pointing to the section she'd highlighted. "It says they taste like pheasants and their eggs have hard shells so you can carry them everywhere and their feathers are so beautiful!"

"But look at their heads!" the Farmer exclaims.

She pulls the book back. "Fine. If you don't want to talk about it."

"And what about the part it says about them being loud?"

"They eat ticks. Lots and lots of ticks—in fact, almost all their diet is bugs! We won't have to feed them at all!"

"...And aggressive?"

She hugs the book to herself. "Please?"

The Farmer sighs. "Fine. We can give it a try."

She squeals with delight and turns and runs to the house to finish filling out the order form.

Two weeks later the keets arrive. That's what a baby guinea is called. They're downy and brown and quite a bit like a baby chick. In fact, you need to treat them just the same—putting them in a box under heat, making sure they have lots of food and fresh water.

They spend their days running back and forth in the box. The Farmer's Wife glances at Hannah, concerned. Chickens don't run. Chickens like to lay around, all sprawled out, basking under the heat lamps light.

Soon their keets become too big for their box. Now, if they were chickens, they would simply set them in their coop and that would be that. But, as the Farmer and his Wife are finding out, guineas are *not* chickens. If they taste a bit of freedom, they'll fly away. They need to know where their home is.

So, their coop is different. It's bigger, with room for them to walk (run) around and room for them to perch, because they will be spending quite some time in there. For two months the keets will call the coop home.

Now, all keets look the same. They're brown and fluffy—until their feathers come in. The Farmer and his Wife had gotten just regular old guinea fowl, so their feathers were black with white polk-a-dot. Many fancy ladies put them in their hats. The Farmer's Wife is not fancy, so she doesn't plan on doing that, but she does want to have one made into a pen. A polk-a-dotted pen would be fun.

There are guinea hens and guinea cocks, and both look just alike. But they don't act the same. The hens lay eggs and the cocks attack people.

They were hoping they only had hens, but there is no way to be sure. You just have to wait for them to get older and see what you have.

And wait they do. For two months...

And all the while, pictures fill their (her) mind(s)...of roasted bird dripping with rich gravy. Eggs upon eggs upon eggs. Pens upon pens upon pens...

The fateful day finally comes and the coop is opened. The guineas step out and look first to the right and then to the left.

Five souls wait with bated breath. Will they fly?

They do not. They seem to know a good thing when they have it. The Farmer's Wife sprinkles grain along the ground; just to help them along as they began their quest of bug-seeking.

They gobble the grain and set off to explore the yard. And the neighbor's yards.

"No! No!" the Farmer's Wife yells as she chases after them.

"Chick chick chickering," is their answer as they retreat to the Farm in a wave.

"Okay," the Farmer's Wife says. "Maybe they just need to learn."

The chickens watch them learn with avid interest.

They run here and there, always together. They chirp. Loudly. Always together. And those chickens must not have left the guineas any bugs, because every morning and night they want to be fed. In fact, they insist upon it.

And by insisting, I mean they peck, peck, peck toes and fingers and legs until the unfortunate soul complies.

The Farmer's Wife watches them closely. Hens should not be acting this way. She hopes. She prays all seven are hens...or six; she'll even take six.

And one day she finds out.

She is weeding, as she always does on Thursday mornings, rain or shine, and just as she pushes aside branches from a bush, what should greet her, but a nest—a nest filled to the brim with tiny hard little eggs. The guineas are laying!

It becomes a treasure hunt. Each of them, the Farmer and his Wife, Mikaela,

Hannah and Jacob, all look under limb and bush to find nests. But they never do. There is just that one. Which means...there is just one hen.

They have six cocks.

They have six guineas that like to attack people.

And so they do.

“Chick chick chickering.” Peck. peck. peck.

The Farmer’s Wife runs to the barn and grabs the scooper, filling it to the brim. She tip-toes to the door of the coop. Six little solders stand at attention at the window, waiting for her.

She swings the door open wide and tosses the grain into the air and makes a run for it.

The guineas let her pass, too occupied to attack.

For now.

Mikaela and her Mother, Hannah and Jacob peer out the window as the troops make their rounds. The first stop is the chicken feeder. Once that is gobbled up, they go on to march along the perimeter.

"Can I get the mail?" Hannah whispers.

Her Mother holds up her hand. "Wait." The guineas move along to the back. "Go! Go! Go!"

Hannah darts out the door. The Farmer's Wife stands by, waiting to pull her back in, if need be.

The door swings open. The Farmer strides in, arm fixed tightly around a white-faced Hannah. "This is done."

The Farmer's Wife nods.

The door opens and closes.

"Chick. Chick---

The Farmer's Wife places the platter down, dripping with rich gravy as she tucks her new feather-pen behind her ear. Turns out they were right. It *does* taste just pheasant.

Chapter Forty-Four: Ode to Chickens and the Reason Behind the Dishes

The Farmer no longer trusts his Wife to choose their friend or fowl.

She greets him at the door as he arrives home from work, pictures in hand. “How about—”

“No.”

“But they’re—”

“No.”

She sets the stack of pictures down and leaves the room in a huff. But, as they say, there is more than one way to skin a cat, and since the Farmer’s Wife detests cats, she tends to agree.

"What is this?" the Farmer asks as his Wife sets down the platter before him.

"Goose," she answers. "Isn't it delicious?"

He nods lightly, warily.

"...and they're not so very hard to raise..."

"No."

"Turkeys?"

"No."

"Ducks?"

The Farmer stands and clears his plate. The discussion is over.

Hannah and her Mother move to the sink to begin washing the dishes. Now, some people have those crazy dishwasherly things, and indeed, one sits here in the farm kitchen just waiting to be used, but the Farmer's Wife will have none of it. Dishes are meant to be washed by hand and the dishes themselves have nothing at all to do with it.

You see, you need at least two to wash dishes, sometimes three. There's the washer and the dryer, and if need be, the one who puts them up. Many and much conversations can be had with a group of two or three. Dish doing takes a good half hour or more, and in that time much can be passed between two souls. Today there is just room for two, the Farmer's Wife washes and Hannah dries.

It begins quiet enough; just water pouring in the sink.

"Those guineas *were* awful," Hannah begins.

Her Mother hands her a wet dish rather abruptly. *Whose side are you on?* She wants a farm just as much as her Mother does.

"The tomatoes are just about done," the Farmer's Wife answers instead. "We need to get them roasted and put up by this weekend. They're talking frost."

She hands her a cup, lighter this time.

"The chickens are nice though," Hannah answers, ignoring her Mother's ignoring. "And Dad doesn't mind them."

Her Mother looks at her. She smiles.

"How about some chickens?" the Farmer's Wife calls out to the Farmer, who has just come into the room. "We could raise some for meat."

The Farmer stops. "That might work. How many are you thinking?"

"A dozen?"

"Sounds good."

He continues on his way outside and his Wife turns to Hannah, who takes the dish out of her Mother's hand.

"Now. What about those tomatoes?"

Chapter Forty-Five: Putting up Tomatoes and The SAUCE

Tomatoes, like most things, taste better when they're roasted. And by better, I mean sweeter, which is the same thing. Some people, when they put up tomatoes, just put them in jars and cover them with some hot water. Not the Farmer's Wife. She coats them in olive oil and sets them a' roasting. There's no length of time you roast them for; just until they're done. And you'll know they're done when you can smell them.

Once they get there, she lets them cool in the pan. At this point they can be bagged and frozen and used later in all kinds of things from chili to soups, or they can be made right into Sauce. That's what the Farmer's Wife is working on today.

Now, about the Sauce. The recipe is The Farmer's Wife's and it isn't. It's hers in that she put the list together, wrote it down, and makes it the same way each and every time. It isn't because someone else made it first, at least she thinks they did.

You see, one of her very favorite things in the world to do is eat something someone has made and figure out how they made it. She tastes. She nibbles. She savors, closing her eyes and breathing in deep. Tasting the garlic. The thyme. And what is that? she wonders.

Most things take a taste or two and she has it, but not the Sauce. The Sauce has taken years.

There was a restaurant not far from where the Farmer's Wife grew up where all her family events took place. Birthdays, baptisms, and funerals, all began or ended at this restaurant. And they had the BEST sauce. It was rich, but not too rich, thick, but not too thick, spicy, but just enough, and yet, still sweet. It was what every sauce should be. And she could NOT figure out how they made it. Days and years were spent making sauces that were just okay. She'd almost given up hope.

Until the day she made homemade tomato soup.

She'd roasted the tomatoes, with garlic besides, all coated in a good olive oil. She'd made the chicken stock, the way it should be made, by roasting the bones before covering them in water, in the very pan in which they'd been roasted, alongside a carrot or two, an onion and some celery. She'd let it simmer for hours and more before straining and pouring the golden juices onto the tomatoes and garlic waiting to be pureed.

And pureed it was, until thick, but not too thick, rich, but not too rich. And yet, still sweet. She tasted the soup, as all good cooks do, and nearly fainted. This was THE SAUCE. It only lacked one thing. The spicy. She carefully shook in one drop, two, of cayenne pepper sauce before giving it a good stir. Slowly, reverently, she dipped in the spoon and brought it to her mouth. She'd done it.

And now she does it each year. Which is a good thing, because that wonderful little restaurant is closed now forever, and how else could her family have a birthday, or God forbid, die?

Chapter Forty-Six: The Lack of a Patch

A word about pumpkins. On the Farm they grow many, in all shapes and sizes and kinds. Well, not all of them can be called a pumpkin; squash would probably be a better word.

"How can we carve this one?" Jacob asks, picking up a small, robustly orange Amish Pie pumpkin.

"Oh, that kind isn't for carving," his Mother says, taking the pumpkin safely away from the darting butter knife Jacob's stabbing it with.

He picks up a Crooked Neck and a Long Island Cheese, a Winter Luxury, and an

Anna Pickett. “Aren’t any of these for cutting?”

“They’re all for cutting,” the Farmer’s Wife answers smartly. “But what I think you meant was carving, and no, we didn’t plant any of *those* kinds of pumpkins.”

Jacob’s jaw drops. “But, but...why not?”

“You can’t make a pie out of those, that’s why not.”

The Farmer’s Wife picks up the lovely Winter Luxury, all beautifully netted and charming. Oh! What a pie it will make!

“There’s other things in life than pie, Mom!” Jacob growls and stomps away.

Other things in life? Is he serious? What can be nicer than a fresh slice of pie? An apple perhaps, or maybe raspberry, and of course, lots and lots of pumpkin.

Sometime later the Farmer comes outside, with Jacob and Hannah and Mikaela following close behind. All are dressed warmly, in hats and jackets. The Farmer’s Wife sets the squash down. “What’s going on?”

"We're off to the pumpkin patch."

His Wife's chin rises. "We have all the pumpkins we need." The gathered pile at her feet proves it.

"Not that kind. The carving types."

Her eyes drop to Jacob, who has tucked himself into his father's side.

"But—"

"We don't have all we need," the Farmer says before turning to go to the truck. The others follow.

The truck begins to pull out, but stops. The driver's window rolls down. "You coming?"

What does he mean they don't have enough? Doesn't he see the pile—the pile that took a whole summer to make?

Just look at her. Standing there. Her feet appear to be stuck in the ground.

The truck waits.

She sighs. "I'm coming."

The Farmer's Wife slides onto the front seat, left open just for her.

The Farmer drives to the Village where the old house sits. There is a farm there, where they go every year to get the pumpkins to carve—one for each.

How did she forget that?

They park and each scramble in different directions, in search of the perfect pumpkin—big, but more important, round. That's not easy to find. Most pumpkins have at least one flat side—unless they're grown on a teepee, but that's a different story for a different day.

"Got mine!" yells Jacob, followed by a "Wait a minute," and "*Now* I've got it!"

Hannah silently picks one and carries it to the truck. Mikaela needs the Farmer's help to carry hers—it's *soooooo* big!

The Farmer's Wife looks at her feet. There sits a pumpkin, just as round and as perfect as can be. She picks it up and carries it to the truck, where the others are waiting.

She leans over to Jacob. "I'm sorry I forgot to plant you a pumpkin."

He looks up at his Mother, brimming over with a jack-o-lantern smile all his own. “I forgive you, and if you *had* remembered we wouldn’t have been able to come here!”

They all look around. He’s right. Some things are better from someone else’s Farm.

Chapter Forty-Seven: A Pie (and Farm) to be Thankful For

The Farmer's Wife surveys her pumpkins, trying to select the very best. Many have already been roasted, their juicy, rich insides scraped and frozen, to be made into soups and pies and cookies and bars all winter long.

But not this one. This one needs to be special.

Not every pumpkin gets made into *the* Thanksgiving Pie.

Hannah joins her Mother. "Watcha doing?"

She sighs. “I’m trying to pick the very best pumpkin for the Pie.”

Hannah nods, understanding. It’s a very serious business.

“Amish Pie is my usual favorite, but what about Winter Luxury?” She turns to face Hannah. “How can I say no to that? She’s beautiful. Just look at her.”

The pumpkin blushes demurely.

Hannah nods. It sure is a pretty pumpkin.

“And what about this one?” her Mother asks in despair. “Or that one?” She points to them, one and all.

Each lean forward, waiting expectantly.

“Oh! I can’t decide!” the Farmer’s Wife exclaims and stomps up the stairs.

Hannah bends down and inspects each one. All turn their best sides towards her. Her eye catches one, off by itself.

She moves that way.

“What about you little guy?” She lifts it up. It’s hard to tell what kind it is. It has a windy neck like Crooked Neckers, and netting like Winter Luxury, and the orangish hue of Amish Pie.

It is the ugliest pumpkin Hannah has ever seen. That's probably why it was hiding itself.

Hannah tucks it under her arm and climbs the stairs and places the ugly pumpkin on the counter by her Mother.

The Farmer's Wife dries her eyes and looks down at it. She picks it up and turns it this way and that.

A huge smile plants itself on her face. "Hannah!" she exclaims. "Do you know what this is?"

Hannah shakes her head, surprised by her Mother's reaction.

"It's a brand-new thing!"

Hannah frowns, more confused than ever.

"It's been cross-pollenated," she begins, but starts again when she sees Hannah's face. "That means a bee had some pollen from a Winter Luxury *and* a Crooked Necker on it when it visited the flower from an Amish Pie! And it made this, this one very unique pumpkin!"

The Farmer's Wife lifts the pumpkin high and its smile lights up the room.

"What a wonderful Pie you will make!"

And so it does. It's scooped and roasted, pureed and sweetened. Cream and very dark coffee and spices are poured and stirred and an egg or two is whisked in as well, for good measure. All this is poured into a waiting pastry shell and placed in the oven where it is baked, then cooled.

The Farm kitchen smells glorious.

Once cooled, the pie is whisked off to Mema and Papa's, where Thanksgiving is to be held. All present come to gaze at the Pie as the Farmer's Wife places it on the counter, next to the other pies, but in its own place of honor. No other Pie deserves such distinction.

After thanks is given and food consumed, all eyes move to the pies, or, more correctly, to the Pie.

It is carefully sliced into sixteen slender pieces, enough for each to have a bite, and topped with a dollop of lightly sweet whipped cream and a dash of freshly grated nutmeg.

The room goes silent for the first time that day as each bite is savored to its fullest.

The Farmer lets out a contented sigh and slips his arm around his Wife's shoulders. "That is a good Pie," he concedes.

She smiles. "It takes a mighty good Farm to make such a pie."

He nods. "And it's just getting started."

The End.

Appendix A
The Recipes

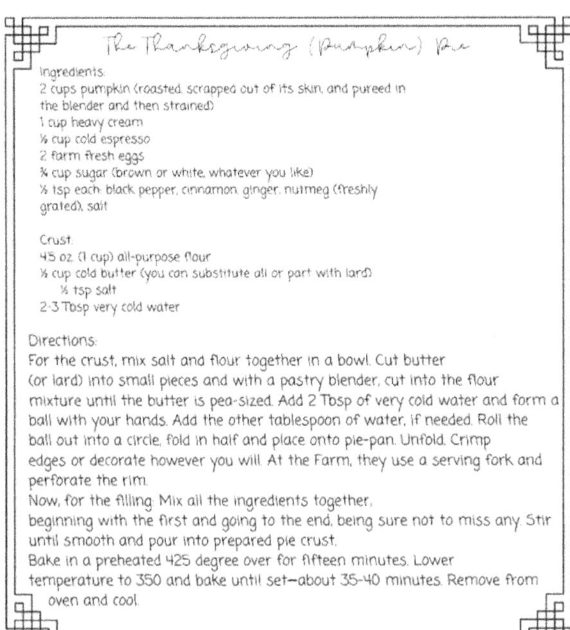

The Thanksgiving (Pumpkin) Pie

Ingredients:

2 cups pumpkin (roasted, scrapped out of its skin, and pureed in the blender and then strained)
1 cup heavy cream
½ cup cold espresso
2 farm fresh eggs
¾ cup sugar (brown or white, whatever you like)
½ tsp each: black pepper, cinnamon, ginger, nutmeg (freshly grated), salt

Crust:
4.5 oz. (1 cup) all-purpose flour
½ cup cold butter (you can substitute all or part with lard)
½ tsp salt
2-3 Tbsp very cold water

Directions:

For the crust, mix salt and flour together in a bowl. Cut butter (or lard) into small pieces and with a pastry blender, cut into the flour mixture until the butter is pea-sized. Add 2 Tbsp of very cold water and form a ball with your hands. Add the other tablespoon of water, if needed. Roll the ball out into a circle, fold in half and place onto pie-pan. Unfold. Crimp edges or decorate however you will. At the Farm, they use a serving fork and perforate the rim.

Now, for the filling: Mix all the ingredients together, beginning with the first and going to the end, being sure not to miss any. Stir until smooth and pour into prepared pie crust.

Bake in a preheated 425 degree over for fifteen minutes. Lower temperature to 350 and bake until set—about 35-40 minutes. Remove from oven and cool.

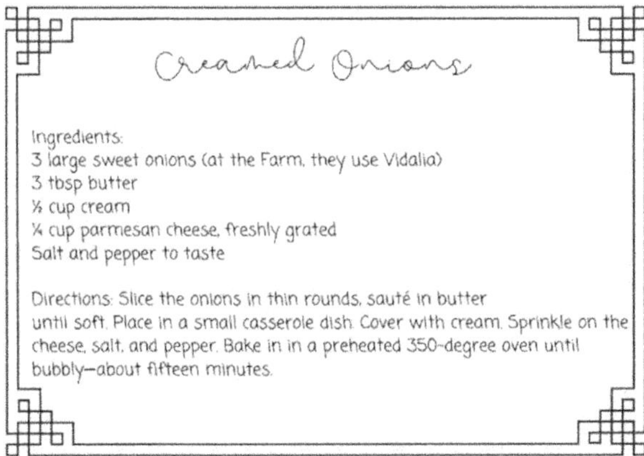

Creamed Onions

Ingredients:
3 large sweet onions (at the Farm, they use Vidalia)
3 tbsp butter
½ cup cream
¼ cup parmesan cheese, freshly grated
Salt and pepper to taste

Directions: Slice the onions in thin rounds, sauté in butter until soft. Place in a small casserole dish. Cover with cream. Sprinkle on the cheese, salt, and pepper. Bake in in a preheated 350-degree oven until bubbly—about fifteen minutes.

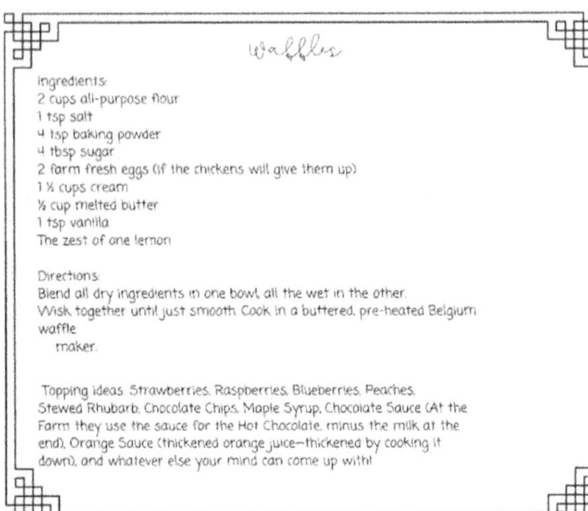

Waffles

Ingredients:
2 cups all-purpose flour
1 tsp salt
4 tsp baking powder
4 tbsp sugar
2 farm fresh eggs (if the chickens will give them up)
1 ½ cups cream
½ cup melted butter
1 tsp vanilla
The zest of one lemon

Directions:
Blend all dry ingredients in one bowl, all the wet in the other.
Wisk together until just smooth. Cook in a buttered, pre-heated Belgium waffle
maker.

Topping ideas: Strawberries, Raspberries, Blueberries, Peaches, Stewed Rhubarb, Chocolate Chips, Maple Syrup, Chocolate Sauce (At the Farm they use the sauce for the Hot Chocolate, minus the milk at the end), Orange Sauce (thickened orange juice—thickened by cooking it down), and whatever else your mind can come up with!

Cheese Courses

IA cheese of any variety or kind is selected. Local made is best. Make sure to take the cheese out at least thirty minutes before serving.

A fruit or vegetable of some kind. It must match the cheese type. With Blue cheese: Apricots. Brie: Warmed Mincemeat. Cheddar: Sliced Apples. Camembert: Dried Cherries. Parmesan: Olive Tapenade.

A Pastry, Bread, or Sweetie. Again, to match the cheese. Parmesan: Olive Tapenade, grilled Sourdough drizzled with olive oil. Camembert, Dried Cherries: a lavender studded scone. Brie, Warmed Mincemeat: Cinnamoned Pie Crust Triangles. Blue cheese, Apricots: Shortbread Cookie.

A Beverage of some kind. In the Summer at the Farm, that is either Meadow Tea, Pink Drink, or Sweet Tea. In the Winter, it will be hot tea, golden milk, or warmed, spiced cider.

Table Settings. In the Summer, on sunny days, this is held outside and a simple checked cloth is all that is needed. A paper straw and a few mason jars for drinks don't hurt, either. In the Winter, a cheese platter is used, and that can be just about anything. A pizza peal, a plank of wood, a slab of slate. Be creative, but try to keep it in line with the cheese you've chosen.

Invitations: If it's a daily occurrence like at the Farm, no invitation is needed. Trust me. They'll come. If it's a once-in-a-while type of thing, send out a card or letter, with a menu and your intentions. Make sure you include a request for RSVP. There's nothing worse than eating a whole pie by yourself.

Decorations. Flowers are always nice, especially just picked. Only be warned, they attract lots of bees and ladyflies. A bouquet of leaves are often a good replacement, and often just as lovely. But the best decoration? A smiling host(ess), just waiting to spend an hour nibbling, sipping, and chatting.

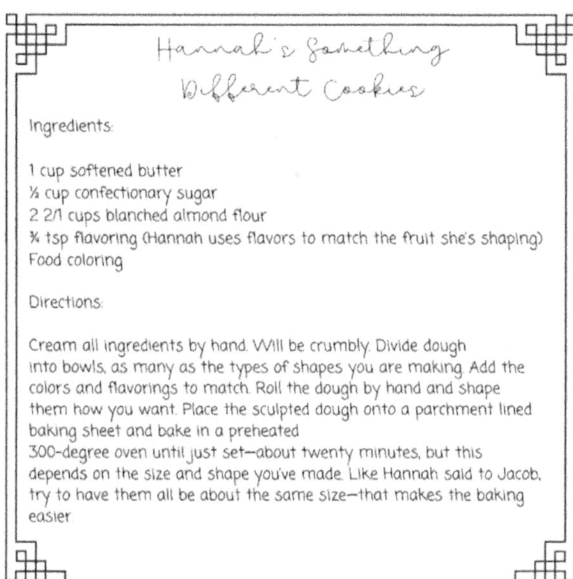

Hannah's Something Different Cookies

Ingredients:

1 cup softened butter
½ cup confectionary sugar
2 2/1 cups blanched almond flour
¾ tsp flavoring (Hannah uses flavors to match the fruit she's shaping)
Food coloring

Directions:

Cream all ingredients by hand. Will be crumbly. Divide dough into bowls, as many as the types of shapes you are making. Add the colors and flavorings to match. Roll the dough by hand and shape them how you want. Place the sculpted dough onto a parchment lined baking sheet and bake in a preheated 300-degree oven until just set—about twenty minutes, but this depends on the size and shape you've made. Like Hannah said to Jacob, try to have them all be about the same size—that makes the baking easier.

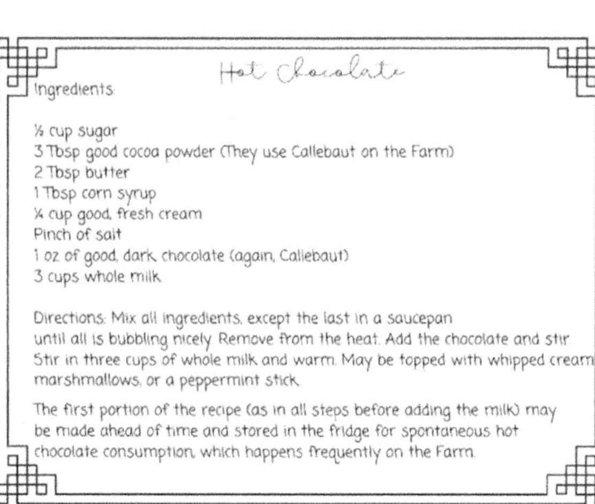

Hot Chocolate

Ingredients:

½ cup sugar
3 Tbsp good cocoa powder (They use Callebaut on the Farm)
2 Tbsp butter
1 Tbsp corn syrup
¼ cup good, fresh cream
Pinch of salt
1 oz of good, dark chocolate (again, Callebaut)
3 cups whole milk

Directions: Mix all ingredients, except the last in a saucepan until all is bubbling nicely. Remove from the heat. Add the chocolate and stir. Stir in three cups of whole milk and warm. May be topped with whipped cream, marshmallows, or a peppermint stick.

The first portion of the recipe (as in all steps before adding the milk) may be made ahead of time and stored in the fridge for spontaneous hot chocolate consumption, which happens frequently on the Farm.

The Nog

Ingredients:

One dozen Farm fresh eggs
2 quarts half and half
Shake or two of salt
Freshly grated nutmeg
A splash of Good Bourbon (for the adults)

Directions:
This is actually very easy to make. It just needs to be babied a bit. Mix the eggs and half the half and half (say that five times fast) in a blender until combined. Let set in the fridge until the bubbles dissipate. Once all is smooth, place in a stock pot on the stove over low heat. Here's where the babying comes in. Stir nonstop until it coats the back of a wooden spoon. To do that you dip your spoon in and drag your finger down the back. If you can see the line where you finger went, it's done. Keep checking it until you get to that point though—otherwise, you've just made some very fancy scrambled eggs. Pour the mixture into a bowl without scraping the sides—It doesn't hurt to strain it, especially if you let it go a tad too long. But no worries; a chunk or two never hurt anybody. Pour the rest of the half and half in—this will cool the mixture down nice and quick. Here's where you add the vanilla, salt and grated nutmeg and Bourbon, if using. Chill until ready to serve. You'll never buy that store bought stuff again.

Christmas Cut-Outs

Ingredients:

1 ¼ cups honey
¾ cups butter
2 cups raw sugar
4 eggs
Zest of 2 lemons and 2 oranges
¾ cup Good Bourbon
10 cups all purpose flour
2 cups blanched almond flour
4 tsp baking soda
1 tsp each: salt, cinnamon, cloves, black pepper, and nutmeg
Your favorite glazing frosting

Directions:
Place honey and butter in a saucepan. Melt, stirring often. Add sugar, Bourbon, and zests. Mix until sugar is melted. Take off heat. Let cool. Stir in eggs. While that is cooling, mix together dry ingredients in a separate bowl. When cool, mix the wet to the dry.

Spread plastic wrap onto your counter and dump the dough on top. Wrap it up tight. Cool for 3-4 hours. Sprinkle flour lightly onto your counter. Divide the dough into thirds, keeping the parts you're not using in the fridge. Roll out and cut with your favorite cutters. Bake at 300 degrees for 12 minutes, or until just browned. Let cool and frost with your favorite frosting—at the Farm, they tend to sprinkle just a dash of freshly grated nutmeg on theirs.

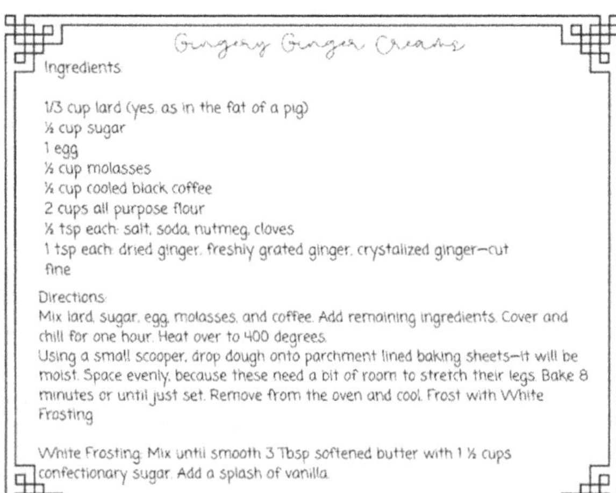

Gingery Ginger Creams

Ingredients:

1/3 cup lard (yes, as in the fat of a pig)
½ cup sugar
1 egg
½ cup molasses
½ cup cooled black coffee
2 cups all purpose flour
½ tsp each: salt, soda, nutmeg, cloves
1 tsp each: dried ginger, freshly grated ginger, crystalized ginger—cut fine

Directions:

Mix lard, sugar, egg, molasses, and coffee. Add remaining ingredients. Cover and chill for one hour. Heat over to 400 degrees.

Using a small scooper, drop dough onto parchment lined baking sheets—it will be moist. Space evenly, because these need a bit of room to stretch their legs. Bake 8 minutes or until just set. Remove from the oven and cool. Frost with White Frosting

White Frosting: Mix until smooth 3 Tbsp softened butter with 1 ½ cups confectionary sugar. Add a splash of vanilla.

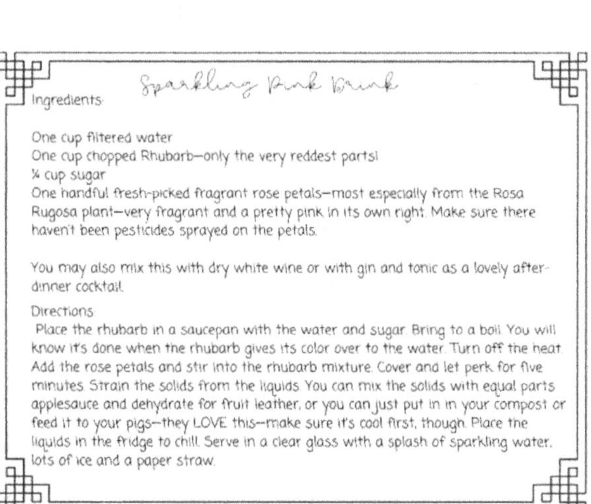

Sparkling Pink Drink

Ingredients:

One cup filtered water
One cup chopped Rhubarb—only the very reddest parts!
¼ cup sugar
One handful fresh-picked fragrant rose petals—most especially from the Rosa Rugosa plant—very fragrant and a pretty pink in its own right. Make sure there haven't been pesticides sprayed on the petals.

You may also mix this with dry white wine or with gin and tonic as a lovely after-dinner cocktail.

Directions:

Place the rhubarb in a saucepan with the water and sugar. Bring to a boil. You will know it's done when the rhubarb gives its color over to the water. Turn off the heat. Add the rose petals and stir into the rhubarb mixture. Cover and let perk for five minutes. Strain the solids from the liquids. You can mix the solids with equal parts applesauce and dehydrate for fruit leather, or you can just put in in your compost or feed it to your pigs—they LOVE this—make sure it's cool first, though. Place the liquids in the fridge to chill. Serve in a clear glass with a splash of sparkling water, lots of ice and a paper straw.

Christmas Biscotti

Ingredients:

2 ½ cups all-purpose flour
1 ½ tsp baking powder
½ tsp salt
8 Tbsp cold butter
1 ¼ cups sugar
2 large eggs
2/3 cup chopped pistachios
½ cup dried chopped cherries
Melted white chocolate

Directions:

Heat oven to 300 degrees. Line two baking sheets with parchment paper. Sift flour, powder, and salt together. Set aside. Beat butter and sugar together until just combined. Add eggs to the butter/sugar mixture. Do not overmix (That's what causes the splits!) Add flour mixture, nuts, and cherries until just combined. Divide the dough in half. Lightly flour your countertop. Roll each half of dough with your hangs into a log—just like you did with that kiddy dough when you were younger. Put a log on each baking sheet and bake for 45 minutes. Switch the sheets top to bottom, front to back. Bake for another 45 minutes. Take out of the oven, and while they're still hot, slice into ½ inch pieces, width wise—you know what they look like—line your biscotti back on the baking pan, flat side up and bake for another 10 minutes. Take out and cool on a rack. When cool, drizzle or dunk with melted white chocolate. Cool. Will stay fresh in an airtight container for three weeks.

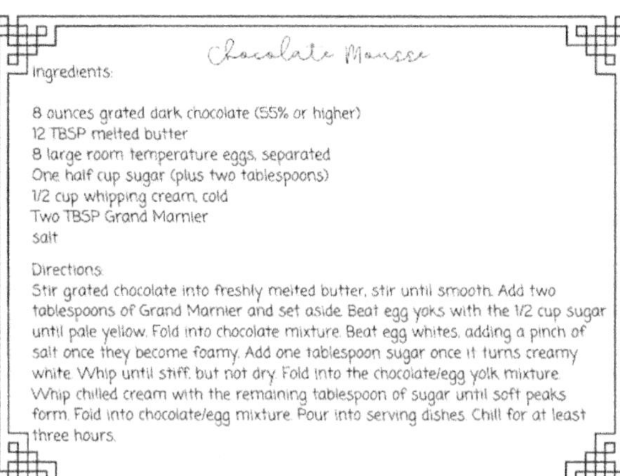

Chocolate Mousse

Ingredients:

8 ounces grated dark chocolate (55% or higher)
12 TBSP melted butter
8 large room temperature eggs, separated
One half cup sugar (plus two tablespoons)
1/2 cup whipping cream, cold
Two TBSP Grand Marnier
salt

Directions:
Stir grated chocolate into freshly melted butter, stir until smooth. Add two tablespoons of Grand Marnier and set aside. Beat egg yoks with the 1/2 cup sugar until pale yellow. Fold into chocolate mixture. Beat egg whites, adding a pinch of salt once they become foamy. Add one tablespoon sugar once it turns creamy white. Whip until stiff, but not dry. Fold into the chocolate/egg yolk mixture. Whip chilled cream with the remaining tablespoon of sugar until soft peaks form. Fold into chocolate/egg mixture. Pour into serving dishes. Chill for at least three hours.

Crab Cakes

Ingredients:

One small red pepper and one small yellow pepper, chopped fine. Two tablespoons minced sweet onion
Two tablespoons butter
Juice and zest of one lemon
Quarter cup sugar
Third cup mayonnaise
Half teaspoon Old Bay Seasoning
Dash of salt and pepper both red and black
An egg
Three quarters cup plain crushed croutons
Sixteen ounce can lump crab meat

Directions:
Place peppers and onions in a pan and cook in the butter until all is soft. Remove half the mixture and set aside. To this add the lemon zest, Old Bay Seasoning, the salt and the pepper. Set this aside. To the peppers and onions remaining in the pan add the sugar and lemon juice and cook until the sugar is dissolved and remove from heat. Stir in the mayonnaise and place the contents of the pan in a bowl, cover and set in the fridge. Now, back to peppers, onions, and seasonings in the bowl, to this add the egg and crushed croutons and stir with a fork. Gently fold in the crab, being careful to keep the lumps intact. With your hands gently form the mixture into balls. Melt butter in a skillet and when it's sizzling, add the balls, gently pressing them flat. Flip once the bottom size becomes golden. Serve immediately alongside the sauce you put in the fridge.

Lockport-drawn by Hannah

Appendix B

I am sure, after reading this book, you are already planning your trip to Lockport (New York) to see and do all the wonderful things described here. Well, I don't blame you. It's a wonderful place to be and live. And to help you along, I've included some suggestions.

The Park with the Mulberry Tree
Outwater Park
Outwater Drive, Lockport – Look for the big, blue water tower.
Lockport, NY 14094
The tree is in a knoll, by the rose garden. The mulberries are free for the taking and are ready all July.

The Apple Farm to taste all the different varieties of apples:
LynOaken
10609 Ridge Road
Medina NY 14103

The Amish Tree Farm where the Farmer and his Family ordered their trees:
Schlabach's Nursery
2784 Murdock Road
Medina, NY 14103 (They ship their trees all over the place!)

Tim Buhr's Tree Farm:
6771 N Canal Rd
Lockport, NY 14094

Pumpkin Farm by the Village:
It's a small place with no name on Hartland Road, Gasport NY. If you're coming from Ridge Road, make a right and it will be on your right about two miles down. There's a box by the road for you to pay--$2 per pumpkin—choose any you like.

Appendix C

Nature Journal Pages

This is my Father's World was a poem written by Maltbie Davenport Babcock, as he took his morning walks along the hills that run behind where the Farm now sits. Because of that, it feels fitting to include his words and his heart as part of the nature journal pages that are following. Feel free to reproduce them as many times as you like. They are yours to enjoy Our Father's World, just as Reverend Babcock did so many years ago.

Date:

Time:

Drawing of what I saw today::

Location:

Observations:

Weather:

How this makes me feel about God:

How this makes me feel about m

This is my Father's world, and to my listening ears, all nature sings, and round me
the music of the spheres.

Date:

Time:

Drawing of what I saw today::

Location:

Observations:

Weather:

How this makes me feel about God:

How this makes me feel about myself:

This is my Father's world, I rest me in the thought of rocks and trees, of skies and seas--His hand the wonders wrought.

Date:

Time:

Drawing of what I saw today::

Location:

Observations:

Weather:

How this makes me feel about God:

How this makes me feel about

This is my Father's world, the birds their carols raise, The morning light, the lil
declare their Maker's praise.

Date:

Time:

Drawing of what I saw today::

Location:

Observations:

Weather:

How this makes me feel about God:

How this makes me feel about myself:

This is my Father's world, He shines in all that's fair, In the rustling grass, I hear Him pass, He speaks to me everywhere.

Date:

Time:

Drawing of what I saw today::

Location:

Observations:

Weather:

How this makes me feel about God:

How this makes me feel about

This is my Father's world, O let me ne'er forget, that though the wrong seems strong, God is the Ruler yet.

Date:

Time:

Drawing of what I saw today:

Location:

Observations:

Weather:

How this makes me feel about God:

How this makes me feel about myself:

This is my Father's world: Why should my heart be sad? The Lord is King: let the heavens ring! God reigns; let earth be glad!

Appendix D

The Lists

THE LISTS

Christmas Eve Dinner

1. Stuffed Mushrooms
2. Clams Casino
3. Fish Stew
4. Christmas Cookies
5. Hot Chocolate with whipped
6. cream and candy canes

Christmas Morning Breakfast

1. Yammy Cinnamon Rolls
2. Pan-Fried Bacon
3. Scrambled Eggs
4. New Day Coffee
5. Juices
6.

Christmas Day Dinner

1. Prime Rib (The Nog)
2. Whipped Potatoes
3. Butter-fried Green Beans
4. Salad
5. Garlicked Toast
6. Chocolate Mousse

Christmas Cookies

1. Cut-Outs
2. Gingery-Ginger Creams
3. Fudgy Brownies with Macadamia Nuts
4. Biscotti: Traditional and Christmas
5. Hannah's "Something Else"
6.

Christmas Activities

1. Decorate CareNet's Tree
2. Light-Up Lockport Festivities
3. Living Nativity at Grace in Newfane
4. Ladies' Shopping Night Extravaganza
5. Gift-Making Party
6. Caroling with Aunt Willow

Christmas Gifts to Make

1. Beeswax Fabric Wraps*
2. Tisanes Milled Soap*
3. Personalized Calendars *
4. Anne *
5. Mittens for All *
6.

Christmas Candy: Minted Marshmallows

Christmas Tea: Rose Hips and Petals, Chamomile, and Pineapple Sage

THE LISTS

Christmas Eve Dinner

1.
2.
3.
4.
5.
6.

Christmas Morning Breakfast

1.
2.
3.
4.
5.
6.

Christmas Day Dinner

1.
2.
3.
4.
5.
6.

Christmas Cookies

1.
2.
3.
4.
5.
6.

Christmas Activities

1.
2.
3.
4.
5.
6.

Christmas Gifts to Make

1.
2.
3.
4.
5.
6.

Christmas Candy:

Christmas Tea:

Appendix E

The Christian Seder Service

This Service was written by Judy Dickinson and used with her permission. All Biblical references are NRSV.

Introduction
Pastor: The first Passover heralded God's covenant with His people and the giving of the law. The Israelites were instructed to observe this feast each year in remembrance of God's deliverance. When Jesus shared this Passover feast with His disciples on the night He was betrayed, He gave testimony of the New Covenant in His blood, which was poured out for the forgiveness of sins. As you follow along in your bulletin, you will see that this special meal is an interactive worship service.

Lighting the Festival Lights
Pastor: Baruch Attah, Adonai Elohenu...
Left side Females: Blessed are You, O Lord our God, King of the Universe, who has sanctified us by Your commandments and commanded us to light the festival lights.
Right side Females: Blessed are You, O Light of the world. As these candles light our festival of the Last Supper, may Jesus light our lives as well. *(The eldest female at each table is asked to light the candles on her table.)*
All Females: Blessed are you, O Lord God, Ruler of the Universe, for You have kept us alive and sustained us and brought us to this season. May this place be made holy by the light of Your presence.

Washing of Hands *(Pastor washes hands in basin.)*
Pastor: Baruch, Attah, Adonai Elohenu...

All: Blessed are you, O Lord, our God, Ruler of the Universe, for You have blessed us with these commandments that we might serve You with pure and holy hands.

The Cup of Sanctification *(Pour first cup of wine)*
MEN: "Therefore say to the Israelites: "I am the LORD and I will bring you out from under the yoke of the Egyptians. I will free you from being slaves to them and will redeem you with an outstretched arm and with mighty acts of judgment. I will take you as my own people, and I will be your God. Then you will know that I am the LORD your God, who brought you out from under the yoke of the Egyptians."

Exodus 6:6,7

WOMEN: But you are a chosen people, a royal priesthood, a holy nation, a people belonging to God, that you may declare the praise of him who called you out of darkness into His wonderful light. Once you were not a people, but now you are the people of God; once you had not received mercy, but now you have received mercy. *1 Peter 2:9,10*

Pastor: Baruch, Attah, Adonai Elohenu...

All: Blessed are you, O Lord our God, Ruler of the Universe, who creates the fruit of the vine, who calls and redeems His people. *(Drink first cup of wine.)*

Herbs in Saltwater

All Children: Why is this night different from all other nights? On all other nights we do not dip herbs in any condiment. Why on this night do we dip them in saltwater?
Pastor: This parsley represents life, which comes from God. The taste of saltwater reminds us of the tears shed by the Israelites as they cried out to the LORD to rescue them from slavery.

All: "My father was a wandering Aramean, and he went down into Egypt with a few people and lived there and became a great nation, powerful and numerous. But the Egyptians mistreated us and made us suffer, putting us to hard labor. Then we cried out to the Lord, the God of our fathers, and the Lord heard our voice and saw our misery, toil and oppression." *Deut. 26:5-7*

Pastor: As God's dear children, we have shed our own repentant tears because of our slavery to sin.

WOMEN: Jesus replied, "I tell you the truth, everyone who sins is a slave to sin. Now a slave has no permanent place in the family, but a son belongs to it forever. So if the Son sets you free, you will be free indeed. *John 8:34-36*

Pastor: Baruch, Attah, Adonai Elohenu...

All: Blessed are You, O God, for You have created the fruit of the earth. *(Parsley is dipped in saltwater and eaten.)*

Bitter Herbs

All Children: Why is this night different from all other nights? On all other nights, we eat all kinds of herbs. Why on this night do we eat especially bitter herbs?

Pastor: These bitter herbs are a reminder of the bitterness of slavery which the Israelites endured while in bondage to the Egyptians.

MEN: So they put slave masters over them to oppress them with forced labor, and they built Pithon and Rameses as store cities for Pharaoh. But the more they were oppressed, the more they multiplied and spread, so that the Egyptians came to dread the Israelites and worked them ruthlessly. They made their lives bitter with hard labor in brick and mortar and with all kinds of work in the fields; in all their hard labor the Egyptians used them ruthlessly. *Exodus 1:11-14*

Pastor: As God's beloved children, we remember how Jesus suffered bitterly for our sake.

WOMEN: But he was pierced for our transgressions, he was crushed for our iniquities, the punishment that brought us peace was upon him, and by his wounds we are healed. We all, like sheep, have gone astray, each of us has turned to his own way; and the LORD has laid on him the iniquity of us all. *Isaiah 53:5,6*

Unleavened Bread

All Children: Why is this night different from all other nights? On all other nights we eat either leavened or unleavened bread. Why on this night do we eat only unleavened bread?

Pastor: *(Lifting bread)* This is the bread eaten by the Israelites during their hasty departure from Egypt to their new life as free men.

MEN: The Egyptians urged the people to hurry and leave the country. "For otherwise," they said, "we will all die!" So the people took their dough before the yeast was added, and carried it on their shoulders in kneading troughs wrapped in clothing. *Exodus 12:21-24*

WOMEN.: Get rid of the old yeast that you may be a new batch without yeast—as you really are. For Christ, our Passover Lamb, has been sacrificed. Therefore let us keep the Festival, not with the old yeast, the yeast of malice and wickedness, but with bread without yeast, the bread of sincerity and truth. *1 Corinthians 5:7,8*

The Cup of Salvation
(The second cup of wine is poured; bitter herbs are spread on bread.)

Pastor: Baruch, Attah, Adonai Elohenu...

All: Blessed are You, O Lord, our God, for you strengthened us with Your commandments and delivered us from the bitterness of our tears. *(Bread is eaten.)*

Song of Blessing
The Ten Plagues

Pastor: Pharaoh defied God's command and refused to release the Israelites. Because of this, and because of the evilness and idolatry of the Egyptians, the Lord afflicted the land of Egypt with plagues. *(As we echo Pastor Duke as each plague is recited, we will dip our finger in the cup of wine and spill a drop of wine on the napkin.)*
Pastor: (1) Blood (2) Frogs (3) Gnats
(4) Flies 5) Cattle disease (6) Boils and sores
(7) Hail and Fire ((8) Locusts (9) Darkness
(10) Slaying of the firstborn

All Children: Why is this night different from all other nights? On all other nights we eat without

special festivities. Why on this night do we hold this Passover service?

Pastor: *(Lifting bone)* On this night we remember how the Lord brought the Israelites out of Egypt with a mighty hand. God slew the firstborn of the Egyptians, but upon seeing the blood of the lamb, He spared the sons of Israel.

MEN:...Then Moses called all the elders of Israel and said to them, "Go and select lambs for yourselves according to your clans, and kill the Passover lamb. Take a bunch of hyssop and dip it in the blood that is in the basin, and touch the lintel and the two doorposts with the blood that is in the basin. None of you shall go out of the door of his house until the morning. For the LORD will pass through to strike the Egyptians, and when he sees the blood on the lintel and on the two doorposts, the LORD will pass over the door and will not allow the destroyer to enter your houses to strike you. You shall observe this rite as a statute for you and for your sons forever." *Exodus2:21-24*

WOMEN: The next day John saw Jesus coming toward him and said, "Look, the Lamb of God, who takes away the sin of the world." *John 1:29*
Pastor: When we were baptized into Christ, we received the sign of the cross on our forehead and across our heart to mark us as one redeemed by the Lord. When God looks at us, He does not see the sin we have committed; He sees the perfection and holiness of His Son. We *pass over* from death into life.

All: "For God so loved the world that he gave his only Son, that whoever believes in him should not perish but have eternal life. For God did not send his Son into the world to condemn the world, but in order that the world might be saved through him. *John 3:16,17*

Psalm 113
All: Praise the LORD!
Pastor: Praise. O servants of the LORD, praise the name of the LORD!

All: Blessed be the name of the LORD from this time forth and forevermore!
Pastor: The LORD is high above all nations, and his glory above the heavens! Who is like the LORD our God, who is seated on high, who looks far down on the heavens and the earth?
All: He raises the poor from the dust and lifts the needy from the ash heap, to make them sit with princes, with the princes of his people. He gives the barren woman a home, making her the joyous mother of children. Praise the LORD!

Pastor: Baruch, Attah, Adonai Elohenu...
All: Blesses are you, O Lord, our God, for you hallowed us with your commandments and protected us by the blood of the Lamb.
Praise God from whom all blessings flow
Praise Him all creatures here below
Praise Him above you heavenly host
Praise Father, Son, and Holy Ghost
(Drink second cup of wine.)
Dinner is Served

The Cup of Thanksgiving *(After dinner a third cup of wine is poured)*
Pastor: Praise the LORD, all nations!
Extol him, all peoples! *Psalm 117:1*
All: For great is his steadfast love toward us, and the faithfulness of the LORD endures forever. Praise the LORD! *Psalm 117:2*
Pastor: Oh give thanks to the LORD, for he is good;
All: for his steadfast love endures forever! *Psalm 118:1*
Pastor: The LORD is my strength and my song; he has become my salvation. *Psalm 118:14*
All: Oh give thanks to the LORD, for he is good, for his steadfast love endures forever! *Psalm 118:29*
I thank you that you have answered me
and have become my salvation.
The stone the builder's rejected has become the cornerstone.
This is the LORD's doing;
It is marvelous in our eyes.
This is the day that the LORD has made

Let us rejoice and be glad in it. *Psalm 118:21-24*

Pastor: Baruch, Attah, Adonai Elohenu...

All: Blessed are you, O Lord our God, King of the Universe, who creates the fruit of the vine, who calls and redeems His people. *(Drink third cup of wine)*

Pastor: We praise you, Lord, because You have indeed provided the Lamb for the offering.

All: "Look, the Lamb of God, who takes away the sin of the world!" *John 1:29b*

PASTOR: Therefore, brothers, since we have confidence to enter the Most Holy Place by the blood of Jesus, by a new and living way opened for us through the curtain, that is, his body, and since we have a great priest over the house of God, let us draw near to God with a sincere heart in full assurance of faith, having our hearts sprinkled to cleanse us from a guilty conscience and having our bodies washed with pure water. Let us hold unswervingly to the hope we profess, for he who promised is faithful. *Hebrews 10:19-23*

All: "Worthy is the Lamb who was slain, to receive power and wealth and wisdom and strength and honor and glory and praise!" *Revelation 6:12*

To access the online musically enhanced edition* of this book, please click on the link below.

This link is for the original purchaser of this book only and is not to be shared.

*patent-pending format

www.ingramcontent.com/pod-product-compliance
Lightning Source LLC
Chambersburg PA
CBHW070608310726
48982CB00001B/13